THE GATEWAY

Also by T. M. McNally
The Goat Bridge
Quick
Almost Home
Until Your Heart Stops
Low Flying Aircraft

THE GATEWAY
stories

T. M. McNALLY

Southern Methodist University Press / Dallas

This collection of stories is a work of fiction.
Names, characters, places, and incidents are either the product
of the author's imagination or are used fictitiously.

Requests for permission to reproduce material from this work should be sent to:
Rights and Permissions
Southern Methodist University Press
PO Box 750415
Dallas, Texas 75275-0415

Cover photo by Jon Shireman, Getty Images
Jacket and text design by Kellye Sanford

Library of Congress Cataloging-in-Publication Data

McNally, T. M.
    The gateway : stories / T. M. McNally. — 1st ed.
        p. cm.
    ISBN 978-0-87074-516-4 (acid-free paper)
    I. Title.

PS3563.C38816G38 2007
813'.54—dc22

                                                              2007030732

Printed in the United States of America on acid-free paper

10   9   8   7   6   5   4   3   2   1

To Joy

Permit me voyage, love, into your hands …
—HART CRANE

CONTENTS

BASTOGNE

My father was there, as part of the 101st Airborne, though he did not arrive from the sky, floating down on the scene of battle suspended by a parachute made of silk. He had been at a replacement depot, following a series of clusterfucks in Holland where he had been wounded by a shell fragment in the seat of his pants. Operation Market Garden, they called it. At the replacement depot he waited to be called back to his unit, Fox Company, drilling during the day and drinking at night. He said they drank a lot of apple brandy, calvados. The dogface soldiers, like my father ... when news of the German breakthrough came, the American armies in shit-panicked retreat, my father had been loaded onto a truck in his summer clothes and sent to join up with the rest of his division at the crossroads of Bastogne.

Time past, as the poet says, is time present. My wife is a scientist, working at the Max Plancke Institute in Stuttgart, the city which is home to Porsche and Mercedes and now, apparently, Chrysler. Chrysler of course owns the Jeep, the vehicle which won the war. We are trading partners now. Part of an emerging global network of free enterprise and friendly competition. In the foxholes outside of Bastogne, while supported by fragments of the Ninth Armored Division, my father's platoon dug into the snow. His feet eventually froze, and in January my father's left leg was amputated just below the knee—his entire foot black, full of pus, utterly devoid of feeling. A surgeon in a bloody mask sawed it off inside a tent and sent him back to England. This, you see, was my father in 1945: severely shell-shocked, a corporal with two Purple Hearts, each the color of a bruise, and a purple stump below the knee.

He met a woman in the summer of '45—my mother—whom he would eventually marry a dozen years later. As for my son, he has blond hair, like his mother, who is Scandinavian. She's over six feet tall and Finnish by descent, a rising scientist who has been given a grant to travel here all the way with her family from her California university to study porcelain and other, more delicate artifacts. With her scientific instruments, my wife can separate the real from the fake; each day she has lunch with scientists from Kyoto and Beijing, Paris and Milan—the rivalry, she explains, is always friendly, by which she suggests without meaning to that her colleagues are each a little bit in love with her. Even though I am not a scientist, I ought to know. Days, while she is in the lab, being scientific, I play with our son. He is almost two and learning to speak. He calls her Boppi.

Everything of value, my wife will explain to you, is fragile.

My father is broke now, as in penniless, aside from his V.A. pension and social security; my wife and I are paying for, among other things, my father's nursing home bills. When my father is lucid, and strong, I am told he stumps around the hallways in his Chicago nursing home and tells people about the rise of the evil multinational corporation, which is naturally in cahoots with NATO. Truth is, my father made a sturdy, blue-collar living after the war. He married a thin, pretty girl who had been raised in the dustbowl of Oklahoma, and who later turned out to take him for a ride. This way, then that.

And today we are driving to Bastogne because I want to see where my father served his country. I want to see where he lost his foot. My wife and I have rented an Opel, another multinational corporation, and we are driving on the autobahn. It is raining now, sleeting, the sky is dark and Henry is cranky. He's been too long on the road. He misses our dogs back in California and my back has begun to ache. We've been in Europe six months now and all we seem to be doing collectively is losing weight. I tried to get work done, writing network application codes, but gave up after I first became sick. And now, on the advice of my doctor, I have recently abandoned my third round of antibiotics and we are driving through the city of Luxembourg.

Look, says my Scandinavian wife, pointing.

Look.

The first thing my mother said to me when she met her grandson was, "Well, he certainly does not look like you."

We were visiting Chicago and had invited her for lunch in our hotel. Henry played on the carpeted floor with his cars. We didn't yet know about her boyfriend with the Winnebago, who apparently was driving a beeline across the country as we spoke. At lunch my wife explained that my father, who was in the hospital after falling and breaking his hip, had just that morning described for us the effects of capitalism. My wife said to my mother, "He thinks it's like cancer. The kind of thing that must grow to survive, even if it has to consume its host." My mother blinked at that, for she is not a stupid woman; she knew we would be picking up the tab. My father, who owned a small manufacturing plant, had finally been forced to sell. He'd lost another finger on a lathe just that summer; now, in fact, she was going to sell his tools to the highest bidder. Might I be interested? To pass down to Henry? She and her accountant had been crunching lately a lot of numbers. She explained to us she'd been unusually busy and that she intended to start traveling, now that she was all alone. She made a big point of that. She dabbed frequently at her eyes. Traveling, by herself.

And here, this morning, before leaving Stuttgart for this holiday, I met with my doctor, who advised me to see what I always wanted to. And Luxembourg City is a pretty place, you've got to give it that, but we didn't bother to stop. Instead we left the highways and took winding, two-lane roads through the countryside: rolling hills, like what one finds in the midst of Pennsylvania. Driving, I imagined a lone Panther tank, running lights eerily lit up, rumbling past columns of American soldiers because the driver of the tank is lost. The Americans waved to him, actually, thinking he was one of their own. Deeply committed, the tank rumbled on, and by the time the driver figured it out—that he was hip-deep into enemy lines— it was too late to turn back. So he drove the Panther deeper and deeper into American territory. Perhaps he was looking for an opportunity to surrender? My father used to describe the Germans in their jumpsuits scrambling from the tank, flames shooting up all around them, their arms in the air. My father had shot—and killed—one of those men at one hundred yards.

"Big mistake," my father would say, telling the story. "They didn't pay attention to their maps. They were lost!"

According to our directions, the hotel in Bastogne is located past the center of town. In the town center sits a Sherman tank, right across the street from the McAuliffe Café. We drove past it to the hotel which is brand new. The couple running the hotel spoke French to my wife. They looked at me with pity, the Belgian kind which causes the mouth to purse, because of course I cannot speak French. Once, in college, I read an existential novel in French, or was it high school? My wife, though, is a genius; she has recently authenticated a palimpsest which belonged to Archimedes, who also was a genius. Perhaps my son will grow up to be a genius? Apparently we were the only guests in the hotel. We went up to our room, which was pleasant enough and could have been in Indiana or Oregon. There was a clean bed. A television with CNN and Elsa Klensch, who apparently knew a great deal about matters related to fashion. There was a window which looked out onto the snow falling briskly from the sky.

This is December, I told myself. There is the snow. Here is where my father lost his leg.

Henry was fussy, and I was cranky from so many hours of strenuous driving. My wife said to me, gathering Young Henry in her arms, "You go out. Have a look around the town."

"Really?"

"Of course," she said, kissing me. "This is *your* pilgrimage. Be safe."

I was a soldier, where I did some things I am not proud of. Then I became a history teacher. When we moved to California, on account of my wife's success, I quit teaching and became a programmer and tripled my salary, but still I remember things I used to know. The Bulge, for example, was not a place, but a description: it is the description of the line of battle—the MLR, or Main Line of Resistance. Eventually everything comes down to geometry, to volume and to mass. First there was a line, then there was an attack, and the line bulged, like my wife's belly while she was carrying our son. A sleek and tender curve, gravid with hope and risk. I remember our dogs, curling up with her on the couch, their heads in her lap, listening to Henry breathe and kick and splash—swimming in his own amniotic pool, heated by the blood of my wife's heart.

Corporal, you might say, meaning *of the body:* my father was a corporal with two Purple Hearts. At the McAuliffe Café, I ordered a beer and drank a toast to the good brigadier general. The tables are covered with linen; the glassware glistens like ice in the rain. McAuliffe is said to have replied *Nuts* when told to surrender, though many think he said something a bit more pointed than that. The Germans called in more divisions. They even sent what remained of the Luftwaffe to bomb the city, and in so doing killed a nurse my father used to dream about at night. Certainly the battle could have been fought elsewhere.

In another city. Another time and place. Certainly the nurse might have lived to marry her fiancé and raise a family.

I write code now; that's my job. The Allies broke the Nazi military code structure, by way of computers the size of barns, long before the invasion of Normandy—cyberspace, from whom no secrets are hid, began with intelligence gathering and merely blossomed with the Cold War, during which I was raised by troubled parents at the dinner table. And sitting in the McAuliffe Café, I reminded myself that I still have a secret. I reminded myself, sitting at my cloth-covered table, because this is what I continue to tell myself periodically to remind myself that it exists. At the time I had not yet told anybody, even my wife. The secret, of course, is that I am sick.

Outside the snow filled the sky and the moonlight which fell against it. Just because we do not see it—the maladjusted genetic pattern, the disquieting turbulence in the marriage— does not mean that trouble is far away. As my father used to say, you learn to look. Outside, across the town square, my father had stood in the cold hoping for something warm to drink.

It's a hard, cold world, and I remember the beer I was drinking suddenly began to taste like vinegar. So I paid up with several hundred francs, nodding politely to the Belgian maître d' while I zipped up for the cold outside, while I tucked in my scarf before heading out the door.

I was raised an only child by my parents in Rockford, Illinois—known proudly by its denizens as the Screw Capital

of the World. My father was one of many there who manufactured metal fasteners and rivets. Most of the manufacturing base has since been destroyed by the Asian Tigers—South
Korea, Taiwan and Japan. In 1945 my father came to Rockford,
then the largest city near his hometown of Freeport, as a kind
of war hero, and he had his picture in the Sunday paper. That
picture was framed and posted over his workbench in the garage, where he spent weekends tinkering with an army sur-
plus Jeep he'd assembled from a kit, where he kept his hand-
guns and collection of bayonets and German memorabilia—a
singed photograph of a young woman he took from the blouse
of the tanker he had shot at one hundred yards. A dagger em-
bossed with the stamp of the SS. A packet of German condoms
and a tin of foot powder.

"Bullets," my father would always say. "Not words. When
push comes to shove it's going to be over bullets!"

Like I said, he was a difficult, stubborn man, spoiled bitterly by the victory of his cause, though I believe at least in the
beginning that my mother must have loved him. They must
have had some pleasure together in this life, the initial thrills
of connubial bliss in which I was apparently conceived.

"Might makes right," my father would say, removing his
belt, and then he would take me into the garage and lean me
over the hood of his Jeep.

He'd say, "It's time for you to learn a lesson."

And this is what I know. I know that exactly one hundred
years ago the world believed war a thing of the past: progress,
it was hoped, had made us civilized. Then came World War
I. And II, as if it was an afterthought, though it was merely

an extension of that which remained yet unresolved with improved technology. By 1939 the trench had become a foxhole; the cavalry, now fueled by petroleum by-products, an armored division. As our lawyer likes to say, do the math.

There was a fundamental design problem with the Jeep. During the initial skirmishes in the bocage country, a number of officers kept getting their heads cut off. The roads were muddy and the traffic threw mud all over the windshields, so the drivers would invariably fold them down across the hood, their faces to the fine summer breeze in order to see properly where they were going. Then a wire strung up across the road would hit some guy at the neck and slice his head off, just like that. Eventually somebody welded a metal bar perpendicular to the front bumper to catch the wires. You can see such a modified Jeep in the movie *Patton*. Now you can also buy a Jeep in Germany and drive around the countryside for yourself. No protective bar necessary. Not to worry.

I know disease is like a wire strung up across a road. You cannot see it. By the time you feel it, you feel nothing else. In the mornings, when Henry wakes me, I hold his hand and he wriggles free, because he does not like to be held captive, and then he brings to me my shoes.

"Dues!" he exclaims, because this is one of his new words. "Dues!"

I love my son. I love my wife. I love my father, and my mother who abandoned him, and I love the smell of leaves in October, and grass in the spring. I love the way after you mow a fine American lawn your shoes are green and sweat runs down the back of your neck and along your spine. My father taught me to mow the lawn. He made me always wear thick leather shoes to protect my toes. *You don't want to be a gimp like your old man.* I am grateful, you see, to my father for teaching me to mow the lawn. And I am grateful to my mother for bringing me into this life. I am grateful for our fine lawn in Oakland, California, where our springer spaniels run in the summer grass while Henry throws them ice cubes. The grass, and the dew which settles there overnight, and my son who will someday be expected to care for it.

My father used to say the nurse he used to hanker for—a girl, really—was no more than nineteen. He called her a tall drink of water. In one of the photographs she is standing before a dozen GIs, an apple-faced girl with blood on her blouse. As I was standing in the snow I thought of her. Saturday night, the town of Bastogne thumping and alive. Teenagers from the villages all around had driven in for a night of abandon and American rock 'n' roll—thrilled to be alive, as well they should have been.

Standing in the town square, I turned my attention to the tank, which has exactly three feet of clearance. Assuming the ground is frozen—and not muddy—a man can safely lie beneath it. On the flank there is a hole piercing through its armor. An 88 millimeter shell, the German 88. Through the hole in the side one can see the guts of the tank, and I suddenly understood why *this* tank had been left as a memorial. Because it had been rendered inoperative—taken out. Because the shell must have pierced the armor during battle, and the men of its crew, trapped, were caught inside, and then the ordnance inside would have detonated. A Sherman, once struck by such a shell, would belch black smoke—in rings up into the sky—visible for miles. The armor would grow white-hot. The men inside would burn alive.

To Heinrich, a woman had written on the back of my father's singed photograph, the photograph he had removed from the German tanker he had shot at one hundred yards. Not in English. She wrote, *With my love you shall be safe and come home to me.*

She wrote, *Ich liebe dich.*

This American tank standing in the center of Bastogne has been repainted to look pretty in the moonlight. The treads which make up the planks of the tracks are an inch wide. Surrounding Bastogne are similar American tanks, demarcating the lines of battle, the turrets now memorialized on monuments of brick. *Tank tops*, says the pudgy American tourist, nudging his wife. *Get it?* My wife tells me that Archimedes used a tank of water to configure his calculations regarding volume and mass. *Ten Hut*, my father used to say, which for years I thought was a place you might grow up to live in. For the purposes of memorial, the only useful tank is that which is no longer capable of fire. My father had a tank pass over him in the snow. He dug a foxhole in the frozen ground by igniting first a grenade, to get the hole started, *dig or die.* By the end the men in his platoon were draped in white sheets to conceal themselves in the snow. They hid in their holes, dotting across the landscape—points of a line—the hills rising before them and the German armor and infantry—those greatcoats and helmets and 88 millimeter turrets—silhouetted up against the skyline. If you were caught by the SS, you would be shot, after first being made to give up your gloves and socks. At night the Germans brought out searchlights, ferreting out the American foxholes dug into the snow. The moon was full, the sky full of clouds, the night lit up like this, where I am standing in the center of a town my father gave up part of his body to defend, though at the time he had no idea why he was doing it. He was a soldier; he must have thought the uniforms sexy—the fancy paratroop boots, the swashbuckling dagger hooked up alongside, the extra jump pay. My father, he knew by then of the massacre at Malmedy. He knew of the rumors of the camps and the stench they cast across the continent. He knew he was here because if he were not he would have been thrown in prison.

They shot men for cowardice then. They shot men running from the enemy. They shot men running, either way, their feet frozen in their boots by the deep, cold snow.

When Göring was making his halfhearted attempt to rescue the Sixth Army, the half million or so Germans stranded and cut off across the Don, he sent airdrops of meat paste, which killed instantly the emaciated men who ate it. Still, the men would lie in the snow in the formation of a giant cross to indicate their need. I think about that often: the dying men, freezing in the snow, and their essential belief that the Führer would come ransom them.

As for the western front, my father once told me that Bastogne is a place for ghosts, and I figure he ought to know. I walked the streets, past buildings my father as a young man would have billeted in, those still standing. During the battle the apple-faced girl took care of the wounded in a make-shift hospital. She was going to be married soon. The men she nursed, her hands deep in the center of their bodies, all naturally fell in love with her. The men gave her a parachute of white silk to make her dress.

The wind was sharp and it was cold. I stepped inside the Dakota, apparently a hip and trendy club, though the building has been there since long before the war. A serious artist's music was pounding lasciviously throughout the room, which was smoky and warm, lit up with candles, full to the beam. I rubbed shoulders with drunk men and women while I knuckled up to the bar. Eventually I spotted a quiet corner and took my whiskey to the spot: I lit a cigarette, took in the view. There was a woman drinking alone dressed in a black turtleneck. She had that pursed mouth, that sophisticated lip, which claims to know more than where it's been and whom she's ever spoken to. Perhaps she was already spoken for. I sipped my whiskey and admired the silhouette of her breast, which was splendid. Were she a nurse, here in 1944, would she have bathed my father's feet? Would she have held his hand and fed him morphine? To know a woman is to know oblivion, which is why so many men are quick to go there.

Eventually I struck up a conversation with three men. They were thirty, twenty-four, and eighteen. One worked in a factory. Another was a student. The youngest, my favorite, was going to finish high school and become a farrier.

"A horse shoer?"

"Yes," he said, nodding vigorously. "Not a fairy. I like the femmes!"

The German military during the course of the war required 2.7 million horses to transport their army, half a million of which came from France. I considered the geographic implications of pastures and paddocks and storage sites for feed. Shoeing a horse, a backbreaking and thankless task, reveals one's dedication to the species: I couldn't imagine anybody making a living at that in the States, and the truth is I was a little bit in awe of this boy, and before I could begin to formulate a reply, his comrades wanted to know what I thought about American women. I explained that many are sweet. They said, and keep in mind we are speaking pidgin French and English and German, that American women are the most beautiful because of their large and bountiful breasts.

Behind them I watched the woman in the black sweater, sipping her red wine. She smiled at me then, which is something that has happened to me in a bar only twice. I took a breath. I watched her pull back her hair, which was short, but a gesture which nonetheless offered her an opportunity to lift her breasts. Her sweater was made of fine wool, and the question in my mind was simply this: does she know what she is doing or does she simply want to adjust her hair?

My wife is one of those women in this world who do not need their husbands, which is not to say she does not love me. But daily she works with dozens of brilliant men she does not yet know much about, which is the great draw of seduction: the wide unknown, the field waiting to be plowed to see what might grow. It is the lingering voice on the telephone; the sweet, earnest promise for glory. Like the German boys, marching off by the hundred thousand to Stalingrad, dreaming of victory along the steppes. It's how marriages and nations fall apart.

How is one to resist? My friends ordered us another round of drinks. There was a great deal of pain in my back just then. I could either drink more or go home and sit in the tub beneath a hot, running faucet.

When the drinks came, I asked, "What is the name of this place?"

"The Dakota!"

"Yes," I said. "But why? Why the Dakota?"

"Because," said the youngest, who loves America most. "Because it is a fine place in America! North Dakota. South Dakota. Dakota! Cowboys and Indians!"

Dakota is also the name of a lightweight truck manufactured by Chrysler, now manufactured jointly with Daimler Benz, but that is not what I was thinking. At first I thought I wouldn't tell them. But the whiskey was fine. The eldest, who worked in a small, local factory, a factory probably not unlike my father's, the eldest was going to marry a girl in the spring, and it seemed important to me that he—that anybody—know. So I said, "You know the war?"

"The war. Yes. The war!"

The eldest explained quite seriously that his father fought with the Free French, though when he was unable to make certain.

"You are a soldier?" one asked, brightly.

"No," I said. "My father."

"Ahh. La Guerre."

"La Guerre," said the youngest, to the next eldest, showing off his translation skills. "La Guerre!"

I said, admiring the figure of the woman in the distance, "My father was with the 101st. An army. Paratroops." I made a motion with my hand of a man, falling through the sky, a string supporting him. The woman watched me curiously.

The men nodded, eyes wide, exclaiming at their understanding. In general they liked to do a lot of backslapping. And now the woman behind them stood, waving to a young, handsome man, blown in through the door by the cold wind, whom she apparently had been waiting for, and embraced him. She kissed him sweetly on both cheeks, and then the mouth, and he took a seat beside her, beaming, holding her hand. By the looks of things, they were deeply in love, and I remember that this particular fact pleased me immensely. Steadfast, I thought. Steadfast love. I felt the whiskey spread inside my belly like a nice, warm fire. It is times like this, when you watch a handsome couple kiss each other in a smoky bar, that I love the simple warmth of bourbon.

"The Dakota," I said to my friends. "That was the plane. The C-47 Transport. That was the name of the plane they came from. From the sky."

"The plane?"

I made my hand into an airplane, the way I do for Young Henry when we are playing while my wife is at work inside a laboratory. I made the sound of an engine with a propeller.

"A plane," I said. "It flies through air."

Steadfast love. The kind to treasure, to keep tucked inside your heart.

I know the story of the girl, the nurse, who never got to wear her wedding dress. The apple-faced girl who held the hands of all the dying young men around her. In the end the parachute silk was covered with blood, her blood, after she had been eviscerated by an exploding bomb manufactured in Warsaw. What I do not know is the story of the man, the French partisan to whom she was engaged.

I am not certain, but I believe my father was a virgin when he returned to Rockford, Illinois, after doing his part in the war. He met my mother on a train full of troops, and she was thin, and dark-eyed, her features not unlike those of the girl in Bastogne, and he must have been bursting at the bitter seams. Probably he swaggers a little bit on his prosthetic foot, still in uniform, carrying to her a tray of drinks. Love makes even the boldest of us drunk, and conversely, drink makes even the walking wounded briefly capable of love. Perhaps they stop in Chicago, rent a hotel room, and screw each other silly in the hot summer afternoon. Look how she is fascinated by the dog tags jingling against her chest. Look how deeply they look into each other's eyes. Not once does she ask him about his leg, and perhaps it is this, this fundamental lack of recognition, which seals the bond between them for another fifty years. My father, descending upon the Holland plain, had once caught a piece of flak in his ass. A couple inches to the left, and would I even be here? Time, and space, and where the body greets a foreign object: this is the great lesson and geometry of war.

That night I dreamed about numbers. The lone one. A woman's figure holding on to a glass of red wine. I saw a one-legged man making love to a woman in a hotel with the windows open wide, and the couple unfolded, and I saw divisions

of men loading onto rail cars dividing into companies—
Deutsche Bank, SAP and Bayer. I saw red blood cells, rep-
licating by the thousands, and POWs marching in the rain.
Eventually I had no idea what to count, and in the morning I
was awakened by Young Henry—my wife fresh from the bath,
a towel around her hair, standing behind him. I studied those
tender lines crisscrossing her belly and considered the fact of
our son, Henry, whom she'd made somewhere behind them.

"Morning," I said.

"You okay?"

"Dreams," I said.

"Bad ones?"

"Yes."

"How's your back?"

"Okay."

She stepped into the bathroom and returned with a glass of
water for me. It's never the dream which is bad but the feeling
that causes you to wake. Later the French couple was surly at
breakfast; I suspected they'd been quarreling all morning, but
they gave us directions and we drove to the monument for the
Battle of the Bulge which is set among rolling hills. The cattle,
deeply muscled and blond, linger with enormous draft horses
in the fields. We climbed up to the top for a view of the entire
landscape.

We let Henry wander on the roof in the snow, and I said to
my wife, "My father had a friend, Lucian. They shared a foxhole. At night he'd defecate in his rations box, drove my father
nuts. Apparently one did a lot of whacking off inside the foxhole. Stress."

"I can imagine," said my wife, though she can't, because she is a woman, and one of the operating precepts of all brilliant and enlightened academic women is that war is a game invented by foolish men to prove each has a penis longer than the other. My wife is one of those who believe war has become obsolete because she wants it to be.

I said, trying to explain, "One day, a truck came—hot food. It came too close to the line and a dozen or so guys ran to it. They were freezing. They hadn't had anything warm to eat for days. A cook set up camp, dishing out the hash, the men huddling around the stove. And then a barrage of 88s hit and the men were all killed. Like that."

My wife watched Henry step toward the ledge. She knew the 88 was that particular and often repeated sound in *Saving Private Ryan,* which we had seen dubbed in German. She stepped toward Henry while simultaneously calling him back to us.

"They were too close together," I explained, following. "Too sweet a target. The only way to be safe was to be alone."

"Uh huh."

"My father was ordered once by a major to take the passenger seat. In a Jeep. The major sat in back. That way the sniper would hit my father and America would successfully conclude the war."

She picked up Henry, who was getting soaked to the bone. It was cold, standing on the roof, the icy wind and wet snow in our faces. Henry's cheeks were swollen red.

"Look," she said, turning to me, wiping snow from her eyes. "I am not the enemy, you know. I'm on your side."

"Only people weren't killed like that. Nobody was just killed. They were torn apart. Some guy gets his arm blown off and then his elbow is driven through another guy's brain. Mortars bounce on the ice and burst in the air, waist-high. What nobody ever gets—it's not the guy dying. It's the guy who lives. It's the guy who actually sees and knows it. That's the part that kills."

My wife said, "What happened to Lucian?"

"A shell came into the foxhole. My father had been sent back to report coordinates for the artillery. You give them the figures, x and y, they know precisely where to aim."

When he came back, there was Lucian, his heart in his lap.

A man raises his arms either to praise God or to give up. I give up, we say, meaning we surrender. *Take this.*

First there was a war, which exploded across the globe, blinding as a muzzle flash on a moonless night, and then there was the baby boom into which I was born forty-four years ago. There is an odd symmetry to that number which comforts me. "Life-shortening," said my doctor. His name was Wolfgang, and we were the same age. He spoke perfect English while his assistant took notes in German. In keeping with the tradition of the uniform, they each wore white. "Plan wisely," the doctor said to me, shaking my hand. "See what you've always wanted to. Give my regards to your wife."

Before coming home we made one last visit. This to the cemetery in Luxembourg. Overhead there were NATO warplanes in flight. What saved my father, besides the sheer grace of God, and the fact of Patton's rescuing army, was the air force: first, the supplies they dropped into Bastogne, and then the bombs they dropped onto the German tanks rolling across the countryside.

Victory, my father used to say, pointing heavenward, comes always from the sky.

It had just begun to snow in Luxembourg. We entered the cemetery, walked past the monuments, and then stepped into the field of marble crosses and stars. They stand there about two and a half feet high, and if you've been there then you know it is a breathtaking sight. We set Henry down and let him run across the file of graves, some six thousand. Six thousand bodies of Americans, there below the dirt and grass. The grass was still green, the snow falling on top, while my son ran across the neatly planted rows of white marble. A PFC here, a Captain there. This division, then that. At the front stands Patton's grave, leader of the Third Army, a man who believed in the resurrection of Jesus Christ while praying daily strictly for an opportunity to kill the enemy. To advance his career, among other things, he invented a saber for the horse cavalry.

Eventually I too will be placed into the ground. I touched Patton's grave to see what it was like. I placed my hand on the white stone and held it there. It was cold, and I rubbed the snow from my fingertips against my scarf. And I thought, Patton was raised in California, just like my son will be. Truth be told, which it often isn't, the Germans would have lost the war without him. It was a war of matériel, not honor. It was a modern war—horrific, obscenely profligate; it was a war America won simply because it could afford to buy its victory with, among other forms of currency, 12 million Russian casualties. But it was the war of our century and it will determine, I am certain, the shape and agony of those next to come.

I have so much I could tell my wife. I could tell her about the dogs. The Russian dogs, trained at birth to feed beneath an armored vehicle. The Russians strapped mines to the backs of these dogs and sent them off to greet the German tanks racing across the Don. After a few explosions, the German soldier simply learned to shoot any dog running toward him. Then he ate what was left of it. He ate the horses rotting in the fields. The fields turned to mud and shit. When the Germans ran out of lumber to make roads for their tanks, they used the corpses of the Russian dead, like planks. Like the dogs strapped with mines to their back, any soldier is capable of instruction.

I turned to my wife, and she took my hands, warming them with her own, and I said, "I want us to leave early. I want to go back home."

"I know."

"I miss our dogs."

"Me too," she said, nodding in the snow. "I know."

"I'm sick."

I hadn't told her I was sick, you see. But she knew by now that it was coming. She knew because she was my wife and had listened to me at night while I sat in the bath full of running hot water and held my ribs. She knew about my visits to Wolfgang, the traces of the repeated blood tests lingering on my arms. She bit her lip and said, "This was supposed to be a lark. I can do my work better at home, anyway." She said, and I swear to God I shall love her always for this, "We'll be safe there."

During the last great war, America got off easy. It never has been me that I've been worried about; it's how I knew I had become a man, once I understood this: once I understood that it was the very nature of war to inflict losses far greater upon the world than anything I might ever hope to conceive. Perhaps my son, sitting on this frozen cemetery lawn in his Gymboree snowsuit, perhaps my son might grow up to be a doctor. Or a priest. Perhaps he will become a scientist like his mom. It's not important to most of us, the things each of us does in this world. Another American in this world isn't going to save the Middle East. Or the economy in Moscow. And probably my son is never going to change the world.

But he might, you see. He just might, if only his very own.

And in this case, might—or possibility—does make right.

I asked my father once why he shot the German tanker who had burst into flames, to which my father replied, "So he wouldn't burn to death, Son." During my own son's birth, I remember our nurse turning to me in the delivery room, explaining to me that the baby was at zero station. His head passing through his mother's pelvis, my son drew his life's first breath.

My father was one of a half dozen men who buried the girl. The men, he told me, wrapped her body in the parachute silk they had given her to make her wedding dress. Once she had brought to my father a cup of tea, and it is then, I am certain, he must have fallen in love with her. He was nineteen, and he had been sent back off the line—four hours, to rest—and he was standing huddled beneath his sheet beside a destroyed bakery, bricks and splinters everywhere, when the girl, having seen him, stepped out of the makeshift hospital. She was wearing only her shoes and skirt and blouse. The wind blew her hair in her eyes, and they teared up instantly, and she said to my father, "Here. For you," as she handed to him a cup of tea. The tea steamed into the winter air like smoke, and the girl wiped her eyes and turned around, stepped back inside her hospital, and disappeared for life.

I should also tell you that it's warm here in California this time of year. My father is now living five miles down the road at the Sunnyvale Home for Independent Living; he has a friend named Burt who survived Guadalcanal and has several teeth he pried from Japanese POWs to prove it, though my father will tell you privately that he thinks Burt traded whiskey for those teeth just to have some souvenirs. My father, who is jealous of these teeth, calls his new home The Barracks and has taken to wearing once again his dogtags. As for my mother, she has recently sent to me a postcard from the mountains of Colorado. Apparently she has her sights now set on a soon-to-be widowed vintner who is caring for his disabled wife. On weekends, my wife brings my father home to eat a decent meal and tell us the same stories. Sometimes we rent movies for after Young Henry falls asleep, movies like *A Bridge Too Far* and *Anzio*. And at night, the dogs, at night just as it is getting dark, the dogs curl up with my wife on the couch, resting their heads on her lap. My hair has long since fallen out but this I am told may just be temporary.

Tell me about the nurse, I'll ask my father sometimes. *Tell me about the girl who got away?*

Blown to bits, he says, every time. *Should have married that girl.* And then he will explain why, as he always does, filling in the gaps of his memory with longing and desire and regret. *Should have never let her get away!*

What I want to tell my father, but never do, is that the men and women we love in this life, they all get away. Nights, while I lie awake, waiting for my body to heal itself, for my disease to bear even the slightest signs of remission, sometimes I think about my father in the Belgian snow. He is lying in a hole in the ground, his feet frozen in ice. His hands are blistered with cold. He is not yet twenty, and has never slept beside a woman he loves, has never heard or felt her breath against his shoulder, or neck, while she sleeps. He is instead lying in the freezing cold of Bastogne—a small town in a country he has never heard of, a town not unlike Freeport, Illinois, the place of his birth—waiting to be relieved, and what he must understand is that it just may be possible for him to survive. Without this understanding then how could anybody possibly ever do it? How else endure the blood all around you turned to ice? After all, he has a good, strong heart. He loves God. And he wants only the sky to darken and protect him from the view of snipers. Then he wants to close his eyes in the deep, dark cold and wake to find himself alive—still whole, and warm. He wants to feel the heat of a live fire. He wants to save his ammunition and he wants to wake in a bed with sheets with that nurse back in the town holding his hand. He wants another hot cup of tea with just a little milk and sugar. Because during the winter of 1945, in the midst of yet another war the causes for which we shall fail to remember properly, this is my father. He is a man, and as a man, he wants only to be loved, so that one day he too might be able to love another even more. He is a man, my father, who has brought me here to find him in the bitter snow and bring him home.

NETWORK

The Land of Nod, according to the Word, was located east of Eden and made of desert. Phoenix, it seemed, had become for her the place to try again—a second chance, hope where there is life, however tentatively, and thanks to modern irrigation. In college for the very first time, Natalie read about mythology, as well as architecture and current social ills. To make ends meet, she was paid to care for the elderly—twelve hours a day, three days a week. She lived beside the university then and had been clean for seven months. She'd left her son in the Midwest, at first believing someday she might be able to buy him back. The State of Michigan had legislated certain preconditions that, given her history, she had not been expected by anybody, certainly not the legislators of the state, to meet.

Nights, she took her classes, slowly at first, one at a time. She bought a secondhand motorcycle which repeatedly threw its chain. After finding work at Hacienda Home, she began to think about a career in social services. She was almost nineteen, and life, she felt certain, could be endured only by way of keeping busy. In rehab, along with her obligatory confessions, she had been expected to congratulate herself for her courage. Change was not easy, people said, even if you didn't have to. There she'd thought about her baby often. Her mother visited and brought a picture, blown up poster-size, for her to pin up on her wall beside a hopeful illustration of the Rocky Mountains. In the poster, her three-year-old son is wearing a new outfit, purchased by a pair of loving foster parents, and in this light, he didn't appear to have anything wrong with him at all. During her pregnancy, she'd managed to keep herself clean, for his sake, and it had now become conceivable he could grow up to be a banker or a clergyman. When she took the poster down, the next day, her mother began to scold.

"You don't love your son? What's wrong with you?"

"I love my son," she said. In an hour she was expected to be in Group. After two more weeks she would be free to leave the institution, complete with a new and inexpensive lease on life, though of course she had no idea where she would go, or if she would stay here in Phoenix, which wasn't quite as far west as Los Angeles, where there was an ocean and a beach. She said, practicing to remain calm, "I love my son."

"You love your son? You take his picture down? I bought that picture for you to remember him."

Her mother lit a cigarette, the third since breakfast. Over the years, her mother's skin had yellowed, and she appeared increasingly on the verge of being diagnosed with something terminal, which frightened Natalie: not the threat of death, but rather its constant presence.

"He's *my* son."

"You don't love anybody, do you? You're a selfish bitch, Natalie. You are a selfish bitch."

The same old song. Now her mother began to cry. Before

leaving for home in Michigan, where her mother would arrive in time to watch a couple hours' worth of television until her third husband left for work, she made Natalie hug her for what felt to Natalie like several minutes.

"This place is so much nicer than the other," her mother said, leaving. "You should be grateful."

This place had been furnished by the host of the talk show *Lucinda!* Her mother had written to Lucinda, who went by Lucia, along with Donahue and Sally Jesse, in an appeal for help. Her daughter was living on the streets, had become a prostitute, had lost her grandchild to the state. Couldn't somebody please help? Because Natalie was fairly middle class, and Italian, as opposed to Hispanic, or Black, Lucia's producers had agreed to structure a show around Natalie's recovery: "White Girls Who Do Heroin." One week after Natalie had been arrested in Detroit, thrown into a tank, and then a state detox, Lucia flew her out to Los Angeles to do the story. She also flew out her mother and her grandmother, whom Natalie hadn't seen since she was five, and a neighborhood friend, Kyle. Her grandmother had aged considerably, and Kyle, who had always been a little bit in love with her, barely said a word. He was there mostly to show support, he said, nervously; at the time Kyle was also embarrassed by his crutches. On the air, Natalie had been clean for less than a week, and Lucia permitted her to smoke.

Lucia had paid the cost of the new rehab, which generally catered to middle-class youths with health insurance; the food was decent, and most of the patients were closer to her age. She'd started at fourteen, turning tricks a year later, had a baby, lost her baby: now she was going to college and doing homework; she was caring for the elderly at Hacienda Home and riding around Phoenix, Arizona, on a motorcycle. The heroin had kept her thin, and consequently beautiful, and she was repeatedly being hit on by fraternity boys at the university—an Italian girl, driving around town on a motorcycle in torn jeans and a tank top. Usually, they wanted to drink a lot of beer, maybe get laid some lonesome Friday. Usually she put them off by saying she had to go to a meeting, by which they thought she meant something akin to student government or possibly even church.

Miraculously she had not become HIV-positive. In Phoenix, she believed the desert heat would be good for her; she cut her hair short, the first time in her life, and began to make adjustments to her persona: no makeup, for example, no frilly dresses. She asked people to call her Nat, which took a while getting used to—a source of constant surprise and wonder, the sound of her new name. She had first been tested for HIV in rehab, but it took her several months to summon up the courage to test herself again, to make certain she hadn't acquired the virus through its diagnostic window. Her lover, an evangelical Catholic named William, insisted that it wouldn't matter, though she knew it would. She'd kept him at bay for several weeks with handjobs and apologies until one night after she cut her toe on a piece of broken glass in his kitchen. He'd searched through cabinets for antiseptic and Band-Aids, and when he reached for her foot, urging her to rest it on his lap, she'd pulled back her foot, insisting.

"No," she said. "Don't you see? I'm not safe."

"Nonsense, Nat. You tell me what's safe."

William soaked her toe in a bowl of water, removed a shard of glass with tweezers from a pocketknife: generally, he was good with certain types of tools: days, he ran electrical conduit for a construction firm. His job was to make certain the current was alive and hot. He'd been around the block enough times to know that it was mostly square—downright boring once you figured out the plumbing, he'd say, which nonetheless always seemed to work. To keep the dream alive—especially your own—what was needed was adventure. Now he wanted to go to Africa or Latin America as part of a missionary group to provide relief. He had friends high up in the diocese who could pull certain strings. The world had so lately become consumed: a war on poverty, a war on drugs, a war on terror. Given the number of people she had been with, the number of shared needles and whatnot, it was inconceivable to her that she could still be safe. According to the surgeon general, the odds increased exponentially just by shaking hands.

"I don't want you to get sick," she said.

"I'm not going to get sick."

"Yeah? How do you know? How do you know that, William?"

"Because I just know," he said, smiling. "You know? Like when you go outside and stand on the lawn? You stand there, and a car comes by, and you just know it's not going to hit you. Could it hit you? Sure. But is it going to? No. The car is not going to drive up onto my lawn and hit me."

"I'm not a car, William."

"Faith," he said. "Things not yet seen?"

Like a forthcoming audience with your treatment counselor, or guardian angel. She belonged, of course, to Saint
Christopher. As for William, he was close to twenty years
her senior. He owned both a house and a renovated airplane.
Weekends, he'd fly her down to Tijuana, where they'd walk
along the streets considering various opportunities to do
some good. William knew she'd had a drug problem—they'd
met in NA, a daytime group he had personally initiated years
ago—and she realized that although he must have had some
understanding of certain elements of her past, those things a
sixteen-year-old addict does to get by on the streets of Detroit,
she had still never told him about her son, or her mother, or
her patron, Lucia, in Los Angeles, who had sent Natalie her
home phone number as well as checks twice a year to help her
with tuition. Lately William had been encouraging Natalie to
move in with him. If he found a mission, they'd have to be
married, at least on paper. Living together, he argued, they
could get used to living a normal life. What the pope didn't
know wouldn't hurt him.

That night, caution to the wind, they made love proper
the very first time. They made love first on the sofa, the light
falling in through the blinds, her toe bandaged with gauze.
She had to be careful not to bump it. She had to be careful
with her teeth. William was expert primarily with his hands,
though certainly she was not about to come. Over the years,
her body had become far too distant for her mind to ever fully
reach. It was something you learned to live in, the best you
could, and it was something you learned to take advantage of
so long as you could use it to bring you comfort. If you fed the

body—smack, an occasional blueberry muffin, peppermint ice cream—it kept you free from side effects. You didn't have to bother with the intrusions of a boyfriend who sold you to his friends, or a cop who promised to drive you home if you were good. By good, he didn't necessarily mean behavior. The body, she reasoned then, had been constructed for the use of others, particularly a man who claimed to need it. Even the body of Christ had been given up to feed the world, each and every day, all over the world. The body needed to be fed because the world was hungry. It was that simple, as well as complicated, and eventually she was caught entirely unawares. She began to scream, because that's what pleasure needed—the right to be first announced, in a dark room, on your lover's sofa. Then it made her angry, this unexpected surprise. She locked herself inside the bathroom and wept for hours.

She had herself tested anonymously the next day, waited dutifully for the results—an appointment she began to postpone: first a day, then lingering into the next week. Thursday, after her shift at the Hacienda Home, where she'd spent an hour reading to a man who claimed to be on a Caribbean cruise, she exchanged the hospital coat for her leather jacket and ran out to her motorcycle in back. She had been instructed to park it behind the kitchen in order to facilitate appearances. The motorcycle wouldn't start at first, and she took this slight malfunction to be a sign of her potentially broken future. Then, quite unexpectedly, it did start, which scared her at first. Eventually she adjusted her helmet and mirrors and pulled out into heavy traffic on Twenty-fourth Street, down toward Van Buren, which she always recognized as familiar territory—the street, and the excessive car exhaust, and the boys and girls, hustling. Waiting for a light, she watched a pimp drop off a girl beside a telephone booth. Even from this distance, Natalie could see the girl's hollow cheeks and tracks in her arms. The pimp pulled away and Natalie turned the corner, paused, and finally stopped at the phone booth.

The girl smiled pathetically and asked Natalie if she'd like a date.

Natalie removed her helmet. She smiled sadly at the girl. At first she considered, as if by instinct, asking for a place to buy.

"You're a girl," the girl said, shrugging. "No matter."

"You need a bath," Natalie said, gently. "You need some food?"

"Makes me sick," the girl said, nervously. "He's going to be back. He's gonna drive around the block and come back and see me talking, he's going to—"

"Shh," Natalie said. "I know." She reached into her jeans and located a ten-dollar bill, folded into the size of a coin. She passed the girl the money and said, "No strings."

"Why not?"

"I just got tested," Natalie said. "You know what I mean? I been clean seven months. Now I'm getting my results. I lost my baby. I got scars in between my toes." She smiled now, turned to check the traffic. "I know somebody who can help."

"Jesus?"

"No," Natalie said, looking up at the clouds. "He's long gone."

"Me, then. I'm supposed to help myself? What makes you think I need any help?"

"I'm sorry," Natalie said. "I meant to do something good."

"Would you please leave? Please, just leave."

She rode away into the traffic, feeling apologetic and inexpressibly sinful. She hadn't meant to show off—a housewife at a meeting, having driven there in her forty-thousand-dollar car, wallowing in some private moment of suburban indiscretion. Riding, Natalie began to cry, which was becoming increasingly common for her. Watching television, reading her textbook mythology, looking up at the sky, she found herself constantly breaking down. Her teacher said the Phoenix was a bird before it became a city; personally, she'd prefer to be a bird, flaming and aloft. William had said she was catching up with a lot of grief, that it was all perfectly natural, by which he also meant her desire to be a bird. It was healthy, he said, all this crying ... *a grieving process*, he called it, as if it had become a way to build something sturdy. Mostly it just made it difficult to see clearly inside your motorcycle helmet. She switched lanes and pulled into a convenience store. Inside, where it was air-conditioned, and cold, she wiped her eyes and bought a pack of cigarettes.

Outside, she sat on her helmet, lit a cigarette and took a drag. The curb, she noticed, was hot and scattered with butts. And it made her dizzy, the nicotine, flushing into her bloodstream. She draped her arms across the tops of her knees. She'd found she could quit smoking on a day's notice, no problem whatsoever. She had no interest in alcohol. And she realized, sitting there, that she had talked herself into finding a place to score. It terrified her, realizing that. Now she turned up her wrist to examine her veins. Her veins were blue and, from this distance, seemed to be located in a remarkably distant place.

"No," she said, coming home, her head in her hands. "No. No no no."

Then a man walking by, six-pack in hand, asked her if she'd like a ride.

Sebastian, she realized, had been expected to fill his body with at least a dozen arrows. Life of the Saint.

The next day she tried again. She read to the man on the Caribbean cruise from her secondhand copy of *Classical Mythology*. He liked the love stories best, he said, shielding his eyes from the Caribbean sun. She said good-bye and exchanged her lab coat for her jacket and drove her motorcycle to the clinic, brushed her hair from her eyes, and walked into the building as if she knew precisely what she was doing. The clinic was located in a deserted mall on Thomas Street. The chairs were orange plastic, filthy, covered with soot. A pregnant white girl was reading a magazine. Natalie was instructed to wait beside the pregnant girl and magazines until her counselor, a maternal-looking Latina, called her in for her results.

The woman's nametag read *Juanita*. She wore the same kind of lab coat Natalie wore at Hacienda Home in order to appear professional.

"Natalie?" Juanita said, sitting behind her desk.

"Nat," Natalie said.

"You're fine," said the woman, generously. "Clean bill of health."

At first she believed she had done something wrong again. Mostly it wasn't supposed to be this easy. She wanted to have a reason to make herself feel bad, if only to provide an explanation for her condition, this constant state of inexplicable sorrow, and she waited expectantly for Juanita to finish asking questions about her lifestyle. Drugs, sexual history, certain preconditions that might have prompted this particular visit—each of which, the questions, were entirely humiliating and required by law.

"This is my second test," Natalie said, finally. "To confirm."

"So," Juanita said, smiling. "It's been confirmed then?"

"I'm safe," Natalie said. "I mean, I'm really safe?"

"It's like a birthday," Juanita said, happily. "A brand-new holiday."

"Easter," Natalie said. "Halloween."

There were no pictures on Juanita's desk. Apparently she shared it often. Possibly, this was a good thing.

"The thing … ," Juanita said, sadly, "the thing about starting over? Thing is, you know you've done it before. Eventually, you even get pretty good at it."

She thought about it all the way home—starting over, which she was also getting used to. She'd been through detox more than once: starting over simply meant you hadn't got it right the time before. At best it was a good thing to keep secret, and she knew now where this line of thought was going. Just down the road, where she'd also been before, and she discovered later that night she wanted to be fucked—not raped, which would allow for martyrdom, and therefore complicity, but instead a moment of pure and simple abandon. She wanted to lay herself down before a stranger and have returned to her a source of probable cause. Pain becomes valuable if and only if you can begin to understand its origin. Being healthy, eating three meals a day, not putting yourself willingly into a place of senseless danger, she had proved to herself she could do all this. She could be a good person of capital disposition. She knew how to behave. What she didn't understand was how anybody could possibly endure it—the numbing ennui her mother's neighbors had mistaken for the good and religious life. Her mother, before she divorced her second husband, had managed to slit her veins with a broken bottle of Scotch. Natalie had called the paramedics. She'd been wasted then, doing even that. Her mother was lying in a pool of blood and Natalie was sitting on the floor, smoking a cigarette, admiring the way the blood traveled. The blood reached her bare ankles, sprawled on the linoleum, before the paramedics finally arrived. They asked Natalie if she was all right. They left the number of a counselor who could help. That day on television, in Los Angeles and before all the world, her mother had complained to Lucia of Natalie's general lack of gratitude.

"What do you want her to say?" Lucia asked.

"I want her to say she loves me," her mother said. "I want to hear her say she loves me—"

Lucia turned to the audience, to allow for commentary, most of which was innocent and sweet, and now a commercial break. Afterward, when Lucia came to visit Natalie at the hospital, the one for the well-insured, Lucia explained that her own sister was an addict. Her sister had given up her husband and her children and was hooking somewhere in San Francisco. Lucia said, hugging Natalie, "I can't help my sister. Your mother can't help you. But I sure can give you money."

"I don't want your money," Natalie said.

"Course you do, girl. What you don't want is guilt."

"Okay," Natalie said.

"That poster, the one your mother brought. You don't have to hang that up if you don't want to. This is about you. This is about you getting yourself well. The rest of the world's going to do just fine without you."

And then Lucia brought in a box full of viewer-mail. There were hundreds of letters. "Haven't had so many since that show on witches in the public schools. You know, brooms?" The letters were mostly from parents and recovering addicts, a couple from high school teachers offering encouragement, another dozen from men asking indirectly for dates. Lucia pointed to all the letters and said, laughing, "This, now this is the power of the spoken word."

By now Natalie was clearheaded enough to find her situation entirely remarkable, including Lucia's kindness and affection. Natalie had watched Lucia on television enough to know that she was funny, particularly when she put on her black act, getting folksy with the audience. What she didn't expect was for Lucia to turn out to be genuine—a woman whose cornrows smelled mildly of sweat, and whose body was strong enough to offer safety. When Lucia put her arms around her and squeezed, a final time, Natalie asked her for one more favor.

"What? Now you want some stamps?"

"Don't let my mother back in here. Please."

Among other things, Lucia was true to her word. She had the doctors prohibit, politely, any further visitation from

Natalie's mother. Lucia hadn't even asked for Natalie to do a follow-up episode. Instead, she gave Natalie her home number and told her to feel free to call. "Anytime, anyplace. You just give me a call."

"Okay."

Lucia said, gripping her arms fiercely, "I mean it, girl. *Anytime.*"

Natalie still hadn't used that number: instead, she carried it on a piece of paper tucked inside her wallet—a last, secret resort. And of course it was more complicated than that; a dissolute life involved more than merely trying to blame your mother. Her mother was pathetic, it was true, but it's not as if her mother didn't have her own and private history. That night, after receiving from Juanita a clean bill of health, Natalie went to class—a night class filled with several hundred students, during which she wrote her son a letter. In it she told him about the desert and the cactus and all the friends she had— this, she thought, was the advantage of the *written* word: it was easier to lie. Easier to cross things out. After class she gathered up her books from beneath her chair, crumpled up her letter, and wandered outside toward a parking lot. The sky was dark and hopeful. The air smelled like semen and in the distance she could hear sprinklers watering the grass. Then it struck her, as if by accident, that she didn't have anyplace to go. After a while she sat on a dry patch of lawn in order to watch the students pass. They carried with them their books and self-confidence, good-looking people with nothing left to be ashamed of, thanks to a forgiving code of conduct and daytime television. To get wasted, to take your friend's lover to bed, to oversleep for class—that's about as bad as things could get.

Sitting there, she remembered sucking off her mother's second husband in exchange for twenty bucks. She remembered being raped inside a dumpster behind an Italian restaurant: there were three of them. When she woke, she couldn't find her clothes, and her hair smelled like garlic. Her neighbor, Kyle, had come to find her. Kyle was newly wed, he and Natalie had grown up on the same block, and he confessed often to wanting a divorce. Often her mother would call Kyle in the middle of the night, and Kyle would go out and find Natalie, and he'd drive her home to his house, give her a bath, brush her knotted hair and feed her ice cream. After a while, she couldn't keep that down: heroin. And then she became pregnant and kicked by herself and had her baby. She lived with Kyle and his new wife while she was pregnant. The new wife was having an affair with a cop; days, while Kyle was at work, skinning hides, the cop would come over and do the new wife on the rented furniture inside the living room. After Natalie's baby was born, Kyle got drunk and hit the new wife with a brick, and the cop showed up in the driveway and shot Kyle in the knee—it took several operations to fix. Then Natalie's mother took the baby, because she insisted on it, and Natalie was in no condition to argue: mostly because she just wanted to die. She hitched a ride downtown; at best, it shouldn't take more than a couple months. Kyle, meanwhile, began cruising the streets, looking for her, his knee in a brace, his crutches splashing through the puddles and shit. After a public drunk, her mother lost the baby to social services, and mostly, right now, sitting on a lawn during a long and pleasant night, Natalie wanted to remember the details of this life. It had, after all, been hers. Instead she could recall only how it made her feel—empty, entirely hollowed out, as if by a knife. There wasn't even any reason left to bleed.

Being an addict, recovering or otherwise … it wasn't meant to be easy. She knew that. She knew, too, that mostly you had to watch out for the past: the way it could contort the present moment, which was yours not to screw up unless you really planned for it. It took good hard work to be healthy, something to be proud of, especially when you couldn't any longer find a reason: simply, it was so much easier to die. She thought of her son, who would be turning four soon. Years from now she would have no idea what he would look like. Probably she would have to rely on her mother to send some posters. Now, standing, she realized she still held the letter she had written, and it made her feel foolish, writing to a four-year-old. It made her realize she was standing in dangerous territory, some lonely place caught between longing and remorse, and she dropped the letter into a wastebasket. She slung her books across her shoulder and made her way beneath the city lights.

The wisdom, we say, to know the difference.

At William's house, he was sitting on the sofa, rifling through a stack of brochures on Africa. He pointed to some starving and photogenic children and said, "Look, Nat, we could be of use here."

She poured herself a Diet Coke in the kitchen. She said, sitting down beside him, "Do you have to have a passport?"

"Of course."

"I mean, a special kind? You know—like for secret agents? I thought all those people were spies."

In Africa, she thought, there wouldn't be anybody to have a meeting with. Of course, the temptations probably wouldn't be the same, either—at least not so easily relieved, and wasn't it the possibility of sin, the very accessibility of it all, which made you hungry? Instead they could swat flies and carry sacks of grain and bury the dead by the hundredfold. In the morning, William said, shifting his weight, he was going to fly up to the Grand Canyon. There was a priest up on the rez he wanted to have breakfast with. The priest spoke in tongues, William said. He was one of the faithful. He was being pressured by the elders to cast his vote for a casino.

She sat back into the deep couch. He put his arm around her and said, "Rough day?"

"Sad. Just sad."

"You want to go up north with me? We could buzz the Colorado? We're going to help with some houses, too."

"Jesus," she said, blinking. "You really believe in Jesus? Son of God, all that. I mean, do you really *pray* to Jesus?"

"Only when I'm lonely," William said, laughing.

"So it's a show? It's a performance?"

"It's God," William said. "Call it what you like. Supreme Being? In this country, Jesus tends to win more votes because he's handsome."

She began to cry, softly, her face in his chest. She realized he was older than her father. She realized she didn't even know where William had been born.

"What? What's happening, Nat?"

"I don't know," she said. "I guess I was kind of hoping it might have been true. You know? I mean, I've always wanted it to be true."

"Of course it's true. It has to be *true*, Nat. How else would we be here?" He laughed, and said, "It's a bit late to try and do away with the Inquisition." He ruffled her hair, the back of her neck, which had been closely shaved. "Just because it's myth doesn't mean it isn't true."

"So everything's going to be all right? Tomorrow's going to be a better day?"

He lifted her face. He kissed her eyes and said, "Of course not, Nat. Don't you see? That's what makes us different. We know better."

She smiled, wiped her eyes. "I'm not sick," she said. "The results came in."

He nodded, not smugly, though he'd known it all along. Because she had a long life to live and wasn't going to be let off so easily. "Those who can," William liked to say, especially over coffee, "those who can, must."

She was afraid to stay the night, afraid she might say something wrong, perhaps even in her sleep, which at this rate was going to take hours to arrive—sleep, and the possibility for escape, however briefly. She kissed William at the door and drove home, slowly, in order to extend the trip. Once home she'd merely have to sit in her chair, overlooking the pool of a neighboring apartment complex, waiting for the sunrise. When the sun rose it would hit the water and set the world aflame—the fine and glorious conflagration of the day. At seven, she could go to Mass, which for a while would make her feel as if she were part of something, if only the congregation—the sleepy and the hopeful, ducking into a cool church, just beyond reach of the sun. Driving, the streets now finally quiet, the air cutting through her jeans and socks, she relished the warmth from the engine. At night in the desert, driving fifty miles an hour, it was possible to chill yourself to the bone. The bike felt loose, but oddly warm, and she thought about the way that felt—the moment when the sun would rise, simply because it had to, because it had become a law. In order to stay alive, to redeem the past, to forgive yourself for the life you were still afraid to take, one day and into the next, the sun still had to rise. Otherwise, all was dark, and cold as rock.

That night she had a dream she died.

William flew up north to the reservation. He called, two days later, to say he wanted to finish up wiring a block of houses. He said on the phone, excitedly, "They didn't know I understood electricity."

In the background, she could hear trucks driving.

"The government built the brothers' houses without wire. Tax dollars, you know. Now all we gotta do is find a decent plumber." He said, "Lights, rock 'n' roll, a kitchen stove. These guys want it all."

"Fly safe," she said, before hanging up.

"Next week—" he said. "Next week, you'll come, too?"

"Okay," she said, knowing she had made a promise. "Okay, sure."

Afterward, hanging up, she realized it hadn't been that

hard a thing to do. Making that promise. She went to Hacienda Home and emptied bedpans. She helped the kitchen staff set up lunch, and after she helped clear away the dishes, she read to her friend on the Caribbean cruise. Several times interrupting her reading, he complimented the captain for steering so well through the stormy seas. Once he reached for her arm, firmly, and said, "He's really a very fine captain, you know. He ate with us at our table just the other night. He speaks French."

"Would you like another blanket?" she asked.

"Oh yes. Yes. It's cold up here on deck."

She closed the book, reached for another blanket folded at the foot of his bed: the magic of cotton, the way it could warm you just so. She went into the kitchen and asked the cooks for a slice of lime, which she put into a cup of water with a pink Japanese umbrella. When she returned, she set the cup on his nightstand, compliments of the crew.

"Oh," said the dying man, beaming. "Oh, bless your heart."

The man was dying, though by the looks of it he had a few more weeks to go. The body could last far longer than the mind, or heart that drove it. The body, it was a wonder, the way it took you places: here, then there. Once her body took her to a park, just east of the city, where she offered to blow a man if he'd buy her a muffin. It had to be blueberry, she remembered that. She was on her knees, begging in a park, just shy of dawn. The snow had turned to ice and slush and tore her jeans. The man, she recognized later, turned out to be Kyle: she had forgotten about the crutches and the brace. It took an hour to make it to his car—somehow, he managed to carry her part of the way. Now he wrote her letters she left unanswered.

To become capable of being loved, she realized, one first had to learn how to give it properly.

Having so decided, she left work early and drove her motorcycle downtown. She stopped at a bank machine, and then a pharmacy, gathering various items—lindane to delouse; soap, lotion, and shampoo—and she explained to the pharmacist she was diabetic and had left her kit in Los Angeles and he gave her a half dozen needles. He was Lebanese and didn't speak English too well, he said. He said he hoped a pretty girl like her would enjoy her stay.

Outside, on the street, she parked her bike and waited for her friend. She saw a coffee shop and sat beside a boy who had the shakes. First she recognized the pimp's car, a white job with chrome wheels and stripes, and she finished up her coffee.

The street was hot today. The girl didn't recognize her. Her eye was swollen—she'd been hit. She smiled at Natalie and expected her to pass by.

"It's me," Natalie said.

"Me?"

"Yeah. You know, the other day? Doesn't matter."

"You like—"

"I'll pay."

"So, yeah. Sure."

"Thing is, you gotta come with me."

"Yeah, I know," the girl said, remembering. "You know somebody who can help. You know Jesus. You know the mayor?"

"I know these motels," Natalie said. "Let's find a Days Inn. A Comfort Inn. Someplace where they let you in politely."

At first the girl was afraid to hang on, but she knew to lean with the turns, and not against, and she gripped her hands around Natalie's waist and said, loudly and into the wind, "I gotta be back in an hour. I mean, he's gonna check on me."

They located a motel that looked safe enough and had several stories of orange balconies. Natalie bought the room, took the key and led the girl around back. Going up the steps, the girl said her name was Sofia. "But you can call me Tanya."

"What's your real name?"

"Changes all the time. Depends. Usually it's Sofia. You know," she said, stopping, "you can just give me a ten and take me back. I mean, if you change your mind or anything. You can just give me a ten-spot and we can call this thing all off."

"Nothing bad," Natalie said, turning on the steps. She took the girl by the shoulders and looked her in the eyes. "You're sick?"

"No. Not yet."

"Look at me. I promise. Nothing bad."

Inside, Natalie ran a bath, then quickly poured in the lindane. The pellucid water sparkled and the girl went to the radiator and looked out the window. She reached for the drapes, sighed, and left them open. She took off her T-shirt and jeans and underwear. She said, standing there, balancing her weight from one foot to the other, "You change your mind, it's okay. I said that. I let people do that all the time."

"You're pretty," Natalie said. "It's not that. I want you to take a bath. You'll feel better."

"You gonna take off your clothes? You just want to watch me do stuff? What?"

"I want to make you feel better," Natalie said.

The girl laughed, as if in disbelief. "What? I mean you're a girl, I can tell you. I mean—"

"No, that's not what I mean," Natalie said. "I'm buying time, okay? I'm not buying you. I'm just buying you some time."

The room smelled like cigarette smoke, which provided Natalie an excuse to light one up. She lit a cigarette and pointed to the bath. The girl was shivering with the air-conditioning. The girl said, clearly making a decision, "I gotta call him. He's gonna come back and then he's gonna be really mad and beat the shit out of me if I don't tell."

The girl sat on the edge of the bed and made the call. She promised double, she said into the phone. Back in a couple hours, maybe five. There was a lot of yelling on the other end before she hung up. Now the girl reached into her bag for her works. She said, "These places, they always give me the creeps. Never stops." She filled the spoon, lit it, and Natalie said, "Hey, wait," and she gave her a fresh syringe.

"Clean," Natalie said. "Doctor fresh."

"I don't share with anybody," the girl said. "Anybody. Don't you like television? You want me to turn on the television? Sometimes it helps, you know. To break the ice."

The girl couldn't find a vein. Natalie removed her belt and wrapped it around the girl's thigh. She pulled it hard, then again, cinching it, and the girl said, "The calf. Gotta use the calf. Nobody looks there, anyway," and the girl found the vein and the heroin entered the girl's bloodstream behind the bruises and she sat there, unable to move but most likely wanting to. After a while the girl's fingers managed to let go the sy-ringe, which dropped to the floor. She lay back on the bed and said, "Hey, stranger."

"Hey," Natalie said.

"Hey," said the girl. "You know someone who can help."

The girl was not quite light enough to lift.

"The nods," Natalie said, remembering.

"Sweet," said the girl.

It took several minutes before the girl decided to make it to the tub with Natalie's help. The water was perfect—safe enough for the elbow, then the wrist, which was precisely the way Natalie had been taught. Her son would cry at first, in the water, and then he would begin to splash, one foot at a time. The girl lay in the tub and Natalie scrubbed her hair.

"What? No," said the girl. "Don't do that."

"I'm good at this," Natalie said. "I've had a lot of practice. Go ahead, close your eyes."

"You're a junkie like me," the girl said, sleepily. "You know lots of people."

"I'm a junkie," Natalie said. "That's the word. The other night, I had a dream. You don't have to do this. You don't have to let this happen. You know? Because I know all about it. I know and this isn't the part that's going to kill you. Heroin, that's the easy part. This isn't the bad part. Getting beat up and whatnot—that's easy. The bad part's what comes after and knowing you're going to live through it. That's the bad part and I know all about it."

The girl folded her arms across her chest, which would hide the tracks in her arms. Natalie knew that people had been good to her—Lucia, who lived in Los Angeles, and Kyle, and others she had known, usually on the street. In the fifth grade, in Michigan, she once knew a boy who had a crush on her. In the fifth grade, she was still good, as opposed to bad: later it was easier to keep being bad rather than admit you had screwed up. She'd learned about it in counseling, but in counseling it hadn't made much sense. You said you were powerless, et cetera, but you didn't *feel* it. You didn't know it the way you knew your own clothes and the way they fit depending on the weather. For that you had to wait for some unexpected moment in a motel room with a television in order to help break the ice.

The girl dozed, naked in the tub, while Natalie shampooed her hair. She recycled the water in the tub and poured in bath oil to counterbalance the disinfectant. She turned the temperature up and sat on the lid of the toilet and held the girl's hand and realized it wasn't hard as she thought it might have been—doing good, providing comfort to somebody you still might any day become. There were easier things, and harder things, than simply being clean; someday, she might be able to tell Lucia, and she understood this was going to become her secret. She was going to take this moment with her first to Latin America, or Africa, and later to all the other places she was going to live. Eastern Europe, the Balkans, years from now. In her dream, the dream in which she dies, she is riding her motorcycle on a dark street, and by the time she hears it coming, she knows she hasn't heard it: the chain, which slips, at first a pleasant gliding sensation until the rear end begins to slide. Coming around an intersection, losing her balance, she understands she needs to lay the bike down gently as she can. She understands that to fail at this is to fail at life. And when her jacket rips, first at the seams, and then into shreds, she knows her skin is just beneath. She can't feel her leg beneath the bike, but eventually her jeans begin to vanish, and what's left becomes flesh and muscle and bone, and her elbow, shaving the asphalt, and she knows she will be unable to wake before she begins to feel any pain. And still there is no pain, and as she dies bleeding on the street beneath a sea of streetlamps, she knows there never will be. The pain is in the living, not the dying, which is why nobody ever understands it. What's left is the body, demoralized and broken, lying on the pavement, and a final opportunity for somebody else to speak. Usually it's William, flying overhead in his airplane, waving. If she could lift her arm, then possibly she might be able to wave back, because it's her dream. She knows this. It's a dream that belongs strictly to the body in which she lives. And to change the dream, first you have to make it welcome. You have to find a safe place to sleep and you need a little time and opportunity and you need to understand the current of the final word … *Mercy. Sweet, sweet mercy* … because otherwise, otherwise you're just a girl, lying naked in the tub, praying someday to be delivered. You're just a ghost longing for a chance to touch the dirt. Otherwise you're just another body without another place to go.

"Home," she said to the girl, holding her hand. "Why don't you let me take you home?"

SKIN DEEP

When my mom asks me what will make me feel better, I tell her nothing. Lacy, she says. *Lacy?* I tell her it is merely sunburn, only a matter of time before it goes away. But my mom is not a practical woman. She believes in the power of dreams, and higher consciousness. She believes she can take away the pain, even if she's pretty certain she does not want to.

George, her boyfriend, tells her she should throw me out. George is an indefinitely-suspended-without-pay firefighter; he used to work out at Rural Metro and drive a lime green truck. The entire summer George has been busy watching out for brush fires, and I have spent the entire day at the river. My boss, and his cousin, and their girlfriends—we took the day off and went out to the river and floated down the stream. It's best to avoid the weekends, and it will probably be the last time I ever go. Before, we went often, but in three days I'll be moving to Massachusetts. Rick & Brad say Massachusetts is a nice place, even if there's not much work. Rick & Brad are like family, and landscapers, and have their own business. A long time ago, my dad did Rick a favor, because there wasn't much work here, either. My mom, even if she never does any, says work is where you make it. Like this summer—I am a Landscaper. At the river we smoked a couple joints, to celebrate, and I didn't feel the sun at all.

The water was clear and cold. At one place, there were kids with long hair and wispy beards leaping from a cliff. There must have a been a couple hundred altogether. Probably, I shouldn't have taken off my top. We found a quiet inlet, and Brad went off somewhere to fight with his girlfriend, who reminds him of his wife, Cheryl, who sells hardware and sneakers at the Smitty's. The tops of my legs and ankles are in pretty bad shape, too. As a landscaper, you spend a lot of time out in the sun, though usually I have more clothes on—a pair of shorts, boots and a tank. Also there isn't all that water reflecting.

We picked up our beer cans, so it's not as if we caused a lot of damage. Recycling, says my mom, is an important thing to do. *Can do,* she says. We also count on it, the cans, for groceries. Basically my mom believes my life's important, which sounds nicer than it is, and which explains why she's so upset. No, *disappointed,* because if you are upset, you cannot be in control of your own *destiny.* My mom is standing over my sleeping bag, because we sold the bed two garage sales ago; she is passing me the lotion, sipping her nectarine and guava juice, and now she says, "Lacy, I choose to be angry. You have shown bad judgment. You have choosed to behave badly."

"Chosen, Mom. It was hot."

"You know exactly what I mean. What's wrong with the backyard?"

That's where George hangs out, especially when I'm out there, too, but I don't say this: her positive energy is by afternoon usually pretty well depleted. Mostly she's upset because maybe some paparazzi took my picture. She worries someday one will show up in the newspaper, at the grocery store, after I've become famous. She says, no longer upset, because she's taken a couple deep breaths, and a big hit from her nectarine and guava, "You got to be careful. You got to be very, very careful."

"Mom, I'm not going to be famous."

"Oh yes you are," she says, shutting the door. Now she is heading down the hall, using the walls, one foot and then another, which is what she always does. Then she calls back, happily, "You better believe it, too."

I have decided I no longer want to be bad. If I am bad, I will not do well in college, in Massachusetts, and if I do not do well in Massachusetts, I will have to come back here and spend the rest of my life dealing coke or selling hardware in a supermarket. My dad is bad, which is why he's in Florence—the Big House, we call it. *Oh, he's staying for a while in the Big House.* It makes my mom feel rich, saying that, as if we actually had a dozen, and George doesn't seem to mind. My dad will be there for another six to ten years, depending on the quality of his good behavior. Before my mom changed her name, she used to visit twice a year, because she still loved him. Mr. Y, my father's lawyer, says just because I never went to class doesn't mean I have to turn out bad. Mr. Y helped me find a college, his alma mater, which wouldn't mind the fact of all my bad grades. It's in a small town in Massachusetts: I've seen pictures. There's a library, and dormitories, and a gymnasium named after Mr.

Y's dead brother, because his dead brother was almost a famous person once.

Mr. Y wrote the college and said I needed a lot of room to grow. Even if he did help my dad, pro bono, he knows we don't have any money left. Landscaping, I'm making close to six dollars an hour, though my mom collects all the checks. My mom worries about the calluses on my hands and feet, the damage from all the sun; she says you start with small steps and practice making bigger ones—steps, in order to build a fine career. My friend Mitchell, whose parents think he is terminally confused, says I'm merely acting out. Mitchell goes to a shrink once a week because his parents don't want him to be so confused. His parents don't know my dad is staying in the Big House. Mitchell says when people don't like their parents, or their life, they often feel bad.

"Hey," he says. "I brought you your mail."

He's standing beside the disco ball we stole from high school. We send my mail to Mitchell's house, because my mother says she wants me to go to Broadway, which really means she doesn't want me to leave home. First I'm supposed to take acting classes at the community college, in order to learn nearby. My admissions counselor, from Massachusetts, who doesn't know that I have lied to her … she says she's looking forward to meeting me. In the letter she says my essay was charming, particularly the part about my dad. She says, *A chop shop? Your family owns a restaurant?* She says, *Your uncle,* meaning Mr. Y, *has requested that all bills be sent to him.* Then she says I'll be on *Close Advising* throughout the first year and we can't wait to meet you, et cetera.

Three days, and I'll be gone, and still I haven't told my mom or George. Truth is I don't want to be a lawyer. Mr. Y said for the application I shouldn't write too much about my family. I don't feel bad because my dad is such a loser; I feel bad because, secretly, I think that I still like him. Of course I don't want to grow to *be* like him. Last month, before she stopped talking entirely to Dad, my mom decided she was going to be a Broadway agent. She says this way she will be able to lay the groundwork for my career. Her cards say *PBA—Pretty Bird Associates* and on the phone she tells people her degrees, plural, are in Marketing and Dance and Agentry. She says Neil Simon has asked specifically for her assistance.

As in Cats? *Never mind.*

Before she stopped visiting my dad and changed her name and became an agent, she decided to build a fortune out of laundry soap. You know, Amway. This back when her degrees, plural, were in Economics and Dance and Consumer Distribution. She bought three thousand dollars' worth of soap, using her sister's Visa, and told me to stack it all up inside the garage. She even bought special shelves which came without enough screws. Later, she said, we'd move into a warehouse downtown. We already had all different flavors, though: soap for whites, soap for colors, soap for fine washables and furs. We even had soap for cars, and shoe polishes, and extra-deep stains. Mostly she figured she'd have the business expanding into Mexico by the time Dad came home from Florence. My dad has a lot of connections in Tijuana.

Once I rode my bike to Florence, to say good-bye, because I knew my mom wasn't going to drive me. Between Chandler and the prison it's all Indian reservation—about forty miles' worth. At first I thought I was going to be dehydrated, for lack of water, and then I finally got there and had to park my bike. My legs were wobbly and you could see the razor wire gleaming in the sunlight.

Mitchell says to me now, looking at my letter from Massachusetts, pretending to read, "So how's the sunburn?"

"Okay," I say, wincing. I turn back the sheet, and there I am, all pink and swollen and sharp. When skin burns, at least you know it isn't dead yet. "Rick & Brad gave me the day off. To recover."

Mitchell puts the letter back in place, in the envelope, and gives off a low whistle, meaning he understands.

I've never had a lot, certainly not as much as I could have, which I've always been glad for overall. I reach for the lotion with aloe vera because I like the way it smells. We have cases of this stuff in the garage.

Mitchell says, "You're going to see the Mobster tomorrow?"

Mr. Y isn't really a mobster: he's actually much bigger and very famous. "For lunch," I say. "We're finishing a job in Paradise Valley."

"Cool," says Mitchell, nodding, looking at his feet.

"It's still really hot," I say, touching my skin.

"You're just a little burned," he says, looking up. "You'll get over it."

Because my mom doesn't want her life to be meaningless, she's decided mine has to become real important, which means if I don't become famous, preferably on Broadway, then she won't be able to feel successful. Everything she does is all for me. All the vitamins she takes, all the clothes she buys for George, all the magazines she reads before she gets her hair done. My mom says when an important man, like a director, takes special interest in an unimportant girl, the unimportant girl should smile a lot and not make any waves.

"Hi," I say, waving to Mr. Y. He is standing by his black car, with the chauffeur inside, looking right at me. Rick & Brad said I could borrow the truck, and I have tossed my boots and socks in back. Now I'm wearing flip-flops, and you can see dirt between my toes. Because it's summer, and hot, Mr. Y is wearing dark glasses and a bola tie.

"Lacy," he says, nodding.

We go into Earl's, which is a bar; there's an autographed picture of Mr. Y behind the cash register. *To Earl*, it says. In the picture Mr. Y is wearing his dark glasses. There's also a picture of Bob Crane, who used to act at the Windmill Dinner Theater, before he was shot. Bob Crane was a Hollywood actor before he went to the Windmill; I don't think he did too well on Broadway. He did play Hogan on *Hogan's Heroes*. When the cops found his body, he was naked, and his motel room was full of dirty videos.

At the bar, Mr. Y says, *Howdy, Earl. She's with me.* He asks me if I'd like a beer or a ginger ale.

I take a Coke, with lemon, and he orders a gin, straight up, with a side of orange juice. We sit at a table in the corner and he says, "Would you like a sandwich? You're all skin and bones, Lacy."

"No thank you," I say, smiling. "I have to get back to work."

"Ah," he says, nodding. "Work."

"Work."

"You still haven't spoken with your mother yet? About Massachusetts?"

"I'm supposed to go to SCC and live with her and then she's going to be my agent and send us to New York."

Mr. Y nods, sadly, because he has met my mother.

"If I tell her," I say, "she'll keep my money."

"Your dad?"

"He says I shouldn't tell her."

Mr. Y looks at his drink, lifts it, and polishes it off. The bar is dark, and musty, so it's not as if anybody is going to notice.

"I have to tell you something," he says.

"Okay."

"You have to listen. Carefully," he says. "You have to listen to what is never said. People, people who …" he looks at Earl, who is a bartender, and nods. "Your dad did me a favor once."

"Okay."

I look at his glass, and then his eyes. They are sad eyes, the kind you tell yourself you will remember, though you don't until after it's long over.

"Lacy," he says, patting my hand, "you can do anything you want. Anything."

"Anything?"

"If you want it," he says, pulling back. "You need some lunch."

"No, really."

"We're supposed to be having lunch. Earl," he calls. "A sandwich. Something with sprouts." Mr. Y looks at me and says, "I'll eat half, okay?"

"Okay."

"Yes indeed, okay. You get some sun lately?"

"I don't want to go to Broadway. Is that what you mean?"

"It's a start. Some people get a family," he says, holding out his hands. "My father built that school's library. The land came from my great-great-grandfather."

"Uh huh."

"Dairy. A dairy farm. It's a small school, but it's like family. We take care of our own."

"I see what you mean," I say, not seeing anything in particular. Because I don't know where to put my hands, and because Mr. Y doesn't seem to notice, I decide to sit on them. They feel really hard.

"Family takes you in. Family lets you go. All you have to do is let it."

Now he slides a manila envelope across the table, around my Coke. The envelope is thin, and inside there's a check for seven hundred and fifty dollars and a plane ticket. Truth is, I was expecting only the ticket.

"You're going to need some winter clothes," he says. "And a coat. Some tweedy dresses."

"But—"

"No buts, Lacy. When you get to New England, open up an account. There's no need to tell your mom about that, either."

My hands are in the way again and I don't know what to do with them. "She doesn't even know I'm leaving."

"Family," he says, nodding. "Don't forget to write."

Once my mom went to a retreat for Surviving Lovers of Criminals, in Sedona, where she met George and changed her name to Blue Feather. Since then, she calls my dad her X and no longer visits him. Mr. Y said he wanted to help my dad because Mr. Y knew more than we did, though he also says nobody needs to know a thing about him helping: not his name, certainly not his reasons. As I understand it, Mr. Y is a director, but not of plays. Instead he directs the state government. He directs the flow of traffic through Nogales. He directs the general direction of a lot of recent foreign investment.

I know a lot more now than I used to. I know that when Don Boles stepped into his car, in 1976, he never expected it to explode. The cops *say* they don't know who bombed the car, but it's not as if a journalist who goes digging into private matters shouldn't be a little cautious. I don't want to be a journalist, but I do know how to read the papers. Bob Crane stopped making *Hogan's Heroes* and slept with teenagers and videotaped them and died in a motel in Scottsdale with the TV on. As for this summer, the news has been full of brush fires, and George, my mom's unemployed firefighter, has been kept fairly busy keeping up.

It was a wet spring. The grass grew, and the summer has dried it out, and now it only takes a spark, or a flung cigarette—there's combustion in the air. After I leave Mr. Y, I go back to the job site, because I still have a job to do. On the street there's a monster truck unloading three and a half tons of crushed granite with the crew all standing nearby. The granite is yellow—Glitter Gold, they call it—and now Rick & Brad are firing up the Bobcat.

"You're tardy!" yells Rick, who is driving.

"Sorry."

"One shot," Brad says, flinging his cigarette. "We finish this off in one shot."

The Mexicans are nodding, because Rick & Brad always buy the beer at the end of a job. There's three of them altogether—Ramone, Manuel, and Joe. Scuzz Bucket, who is an ex-con from New York, is picking at a new tattoo. Then there's me.

Because it's my last day, I want to do a nice job. The Mexicans line up the wheelbarrows, three of them real tight, and Rick drops the first load. The barrows fill up, full, granite pouring over the sides, and then Rick does a little wheelie with the Bobcat, and Brad yells, "Go. Let's fucking go!" and the Mexicans are haulin' ass, and now I've got my square point. It takes a while to get the feel, the way you tilt the wrist, flipping it just so. If you do it right, the granite floats out in a fan. Mostly, it's all in the shoulders and legs, the wrist. Meanwhile, I'm on point, with Scuzz Bucket, and Brad, and the granite keeps pouring in, and this is something I know I'm pretty good at. Not that I want to turn it into a career, but even so, it's nice to know the way ground cover works. It's nice to hold a shovel in your hands and know you know exactly what you're doing with it. It's nice to know the guys don't mind your noticing the way they stumble, lifting the wheelbarrows, one after another. Because it's hot, and brutal, and mostly what I'm thinking about is college, and carrying around my books in Massachusetts, where there's going to be a lot of ice and snow. Maybe I'll hang out in the library and read a lot and become whatever it is I'm supposed to be. Mostly, I don't want to be related to my parents, even if my dad says he understands, and now I'm thinking about the sun, the way it lights up all the dust, and the heat, and the way I'm not even tired. I'm thinking about the shovel in my hands and the way the sun feels so good and hot and the way I know I'm going to miss it.

We are the downwardly mobile. The only thing we still own for sure is our house, but the property taxes keep going up, and sooner or later my mom is going to sell the house, too. She's already borrowed twice on my life insurance policy. Every two months, she holds another garage sale. There's hardly any furniture left at all and my mom says she still needs my paycheck to jump-start the business. She means the Agent Business, not the Soap Business. She still owes her sister three thousand dollars for all the leftover laundry soap in the garage. Sometimes she goes to special seminars: "How to Think Right and Live"; "Vitamins for Success and Beauty." We have two phone lines, a post office box, and a fax machine, but we do not have a couch. Once my mom went to Canada to learn how to write screenplays. At night, when George is home, I hear them in the living room.

My dad, before he moved into the Big House, owned a body shop. When the last recession came, people stopped getting their cars fixed, so he turned it into a Chop Shop. There were still some real customers, but mostly he was into felony and fraud and stolen vehicles. Then he started stealing people's cars—not *real* stealing. Some guy can't make his car payment, he makes an arrangement with my dad: leaves a couple hundred under the floor mat, and my dad steals the car for him. He chops up the parts, mixes them up, does a quick paint job and ditches the car in Tijuana or Las Vegas. Thing is, my dad stole the wrong car. He stole the mayor's.

Actually it belonged to his wife, and the mayor was up for reelection. My dad knew something was wrong when he couldn't find a check under the mat. The parking garage had a video camera. At the door, when the cops came, they were nice and didn't use any handcuffs. My dad had stolen a lot of cars, even one belonging to a cop, who still was grateful. Of course, I didn't know my dad was a crook. I thought he liked to go fishing. You know, in Mexico. I thought he liked his weekends off since things seemed so busy at the shop. The last thing he said to my mom as a free man was, "Do not sell the house."

Apparently, he had put it in her name a long time ago, just in case. Later a group of federal agents with ties came over and tore the place apart—the kitchen, the laundry room. They went through my underwear drawer, and my CD collection, and the crawl space. Afterward, they came up with close to fourteen thousand in cash, and my mom said it was hers. She'd been skimming off the groceries. To save for Christmas, she said.

"It's supposed to be a surprise!"

She did a pretty good job, screaming and crying. There were people from Chicago and Denver and L.A., all of whom came in to testify. My dad, at the trial, said he was sorry and wore a conservative suit. Mr. Y put his best junior partner on the case, which helped a little, but it was still big news. Before, the biggest news was Don Boles, who blew up, and then Bob Crane, shot diddling with himself while watching his home movies, and then my dad went to prison for stealing the car which just happened to belong to the wife of the mayor who was tough on crime. After, the wife didn't want it back, because it was dirty, she said, and a huge man with big chains took my dad out of the courtroom and Mom started taking a correspondence course in Real Estate. Mostly, I remember the newspeople, saying they'd put another bad man behind bars. Bad, they said. The streets are safer now.

I was about to turn ten. The police called it a sting operation. Sometimes, when I used to visit my dad, I'd bring him cigarettes and magazines.

At nine George fires up the VCR—*Buns of Steel*—and I ride my bike over to Mitchell's and change my clothes there. Then we get in his car and drive through Central. Later we go other places. We go to the Incognito Lounge, and other places, because certain types of bars are better than others. The music is fast and people don't pinch you on the ass and everybody dances all together. I like to dance, but I don't want to go to Broadway. Before, when my family was normal, and happy, I was on *Star Search*. I made it to the semifinals and wore a green and red costume and lost to an acrobatic family from Scandinavia. There were more of them, smiling, than there were of me. Ed McMahon had the shakes and forgot my name, introducing me, and had to check his cue card: this is the only time I've ever been to California. We drove there in a van my dad was customizing for a dealer, who said he didn't mind so long as we disconnected the speedometer cable, and my dad showed me how to do that, too. It's not as tricky as you'd think. My dad said he was considering buying one for Mom, for all the shopping, and because of the way it looked so neat.

At one place, Mitchell and I get some drinks. He's flirting with a boy in purple. Before, Mitchell and I used to date, and we'd go out cruising, like this, and sometimes we'd practice. We'd drive out to Seven Springs and park under the stars and undo our jeans and see who's who. Once, I got him off, in the car, and he started crying. He said he didn't know what was wrong. Of course, nothing was *wrong*, just different.

"You won't like me anymore," he said.

There was sperm all over my sweatshirt and wrist, and he was ashamed, and I held him and said it was okay. I said I love the way that smells, sperm—like gasoline, prettier than it tastes. I said he was my friend and he said he was and we took an oath and started laughing. Him first, because it seemed so stupid. We were in his tiny car and the windows were all fogged up and before, the only thing I ever worried about keeping secret was the fact that I had lost to a bunch of Scandinavian people on *Star Search* when I was eight years old, and then the fact that my father was a crook, but I had never thought about having to keep a secret for my friend. Because it wasn't a secret for me. It was a secret for him, and not for anybody else, and it made me feel responsible and important.

"This just makes it easier," I said.

"I know," he said, wiping his eyes. "I know."

Then we went out dancing. Usually he told me about his dates—"encounters," he called them. I never had many all by myself, mostly because I wasn't sure just what I wanted. One guy at school dumped me for a cheerleader, which was okay. She had pretty long hair and green eyes. Later she dumped him, for somebody else, and I started hanging out with Mitchell. A few times I slept with Brad, last June, when he was fighting with his wife. He was drunk most of the time and tired from working all day in the sun. I also knew his girlfriend, and she was sweet and didn't know as much as I did, especially about Brad. But Mitchell is the only person I think I have ever loved, and even if it isn't ever going to work, sometimes I used to hope that we'd get married. A long time from now, of course. After I went to college.

"Hey, Lace," he says to me, holding out his hand.

We are in a club in Tempe by the university. Mostly it's full of college students and married men. On the ceiling is a disco ball just like the one we stole from high school, and I'm trying really hard to stand still and not think about my future. Mostly I feel wrong inside and scared. Inside Mitchell's palm are two tiny pills.

"Ritalin," he says. "Very clean."

I pop the speed, because I want it, and he says, "Hey, what's wrong?"

"Happy tears," I say.

"In Massachusetts," he says. "You think maybe I can visit?"

"First I have to get there."

"Jesus, Lace. You're halfway home."

"I want to dance," I say, taking his hand. "Not alone."

It was Mitchell's idea to steal the disco ball. "For your room," he said. "It will look nice."

When I rode my bike to visit my dad, at the Big House, I knew this was important. Two guards frisked me, slowly, and after finishing with me they went through my backpack. I was tired and hot and had to drink a lot of water, and they sent me into the room, the special room for certain convicts, the one with all the Plexiglas and telephones. My dad had lost more weight and I slid him the cigarettes and magazines—a *Penthouse* and two Victoria's Secret catalogues and the *Sports Illustrated* swimsuit issue.

"Thanks," he said.

My dad, wearing all that blue, looked different. Before he was a crook, he'd wear jeans or army pants on weekends, sometimes a jacket when we went out to dinner, and now he looked like everybody else behind the Plexiglas. He could have been a murderer or drug czar.

"It's okay."

"You look pale," he said.

"I rode my bike. It's a long way."

"Blue Feather," he said, folding his hands. "How's Blue—"

"She doesn't know. George lost his job. He wants her to sell the house."

"She's going to, isn't she."

It wasn't really a question, which he must have realized. A man came into the room and sat beside my dad's booth. He was young and had a toothpick in his mouth, and he sat there quietly, looking at the phone.

"Dad," I said. "I want to go to college, and Mr.—"

"I know. I know." He couldn't light a cigarette, because of the No Smoking laws. He packed one on the counter and said, "Don't tell your mom."

"She's going to have to find out. She's going—"

"Lacy, your mother is a sweet woman. She is sweet. But you do not have to grow up to be like her."

"She's become an agent. For actors."

"Go to Massachusetts," my dad said. "Say hey to Rick & Brad."

After a while we didn't have much to say. He asked me if I had any dates. He asked me if George ever hit me. He said, leafing through one of the catalogues, "Any questions?"

"No," I said. "No wait. In the army …"

"Yes?"

"What did you do in the army, Dad?"

He puffed on his cigarette, as if it were lit, and said, "A lot of things, Lace. I used to do a lot of things."

He left first, as usual. When he got up to go, he waved to me. The man sitting beside him nodded politely, and he turned to me, as if I were his girlfriend or wife. The man was sitting behind the Plexiglas, and he stood up, slid over to the place where my father had been, and tucked his body into the booth. Meanwhile, my dad waved and stepped through an iron doorway, the magazines rolled up in his hand, and the man in the booth across from me reached into his pants. He was already hard, as if he were about to build something with a hammer and a board: his arm was full of knots, I remember that. He undid his fly, stroked himself once, twice, and came all over the tabletop. He stood looking at me, and reached for the phone, as if he had something more to say, and I went out into the lobby and cried for half an hour. I called up Mitchell, collect, and asked him to come pick me up. I took my bike and walked it to the edge of the prison highway and sat on a rock. There were visitors—ladies with their kids—driving by, going back to Phoenix. A couple people stopped to ask if I was okay, and eventually Mitchell showed up, and we took off my front wheel and put the bike inside his small car and then we drove home.

"How's your dad," Mitchell said, driving home.

"I don't know."

We left Tempe near two in the morning, driving, listening to the stereo. Mitchell talked a lot about what he was going to do in college in California. He talked about the way he was going to miss his shrink, and me, and he wondered what we'd be like if we hadn't known each other.

"You know," he said, driving, "if we'd lived in different places."

"You mean if we were different people," I said.

"Yeah," he said. "If we were different people."

It made me feel dizzy, thinking that way, because it was impossible. I just knew I did not want to be bad, and after a while we ended up near Carefree. We were driving fast and then we saw the smoke, and the light from the smoke, rising into the sky.

There were a few cars pulled over to the side of the road, and you could see the entire field, glowing. The fire was in a huge field behind a subdivision and there was a man with a pickup truck, full of shovels and picks, and there were lots of people in their pajamas. We each grabbed a shovel and started work on the fire while two people with garden hoses sprayed their rooftops. After a while the fire department came, with even bigger hoses, and Mitchell and I kept digging at the fire. I taught him to use the wrist, not his back, to spread the dirt over the flames because you kill a fire by covering it with what it burns—by giving it precisely what it needs—and you could see us, maybe fifty or sixty by the end, shoveling and shoveling. The fire was loud, roaring, like the ocean or an animal, or a natural disaster, and sometimes I'd feel it burning, my eyebrows, and the skin on my hands. You'd never think something so pretty could be so hot, or dangerous, and the air was full of smoke, and it was hot, too, but somehow never hot enough to kill us. It wasn't going to kill us, at least this time, because we were so many, even if it was past curfew, and because there weren't any trees big enough to burn: just leftover grass from an unusually wet spring.

Then I thought my father must have thought the same things: breaking the law, stealing a car here, maybe wiring another there—he must have known a lot about demolition. He must have known why Don Boles had gone up in flames, and even if he didn't do it—even if my father did not kill the most important journalist in all of Phoenix—I knew then that he could have. I knew that he could have done what anybody told him to: there was a lot of heat nearby and the world was becoming dangerous and my father was a crook. My father was a crook and I was doing a lot of speed and eventually the flames began to fall away. The sky darkened and after a while I could barely see what I was doing, and when we were all done, after all the fire trucks but one had gone away, a man said thank you as he shook my hand. He was standing in his pajamas and cowboy boots beside the pickup truck full of shovels and picks. His pajamas were streaked with dirt, and now he was shaking Mitchell's hand, and Mitchell said, "Hey. It's cool."

"We could have lost everything," the man said. "Everything."

My dad never did come clean. Before the cops came, he told me once he thought his was the kind of life best kept in the dark. He said, looking down at me, "You know, the kind nobody ever knows too much about. Behind the scenes, Lace."

This was before I was bad. Usually, when my dad came home from work, we watched *Hogan's Heroes*, while my mom made dinner. My mom had decided to be a chef then; her degrees, plural, were in Home Economics, Dance, and French Cuisine. Now it had been years since she turned on the stove. When Mitchell dropped me off at home, he said for me to take my time.

I went inside while Mitchell stayed in the driveway, the engine running. Inside, my mom and George were asleep on the living room floor, where the sofa should have been, the TV all full of snow, and I decided I wasn't going to take much. The sun was rising, and you could hear a couple birds, chirping. On the answering machine was a message for Ms. Blue Feather from a man named Thunder Storm. I poured myself a soda and went to my room to pack.

I took my hiking boots and dictionary and sleeping bag. I took two sweaters, most of my underwear, two pairs of jeans and a skirt. I took three pens, an engraved mechanical pencil, my best eraser, and I took a picture of my dad and me. In it we are standing beside the neat van he borrowed somewhere on the highway to California: I am wearing my dance outfit, and his arm is around me, and you can tell he's happy even if I lost. Then I went into the bathroom and I packed my shampoo and toothbrush and a small box of concentrated laundry detergent for fine washables. I didn't leave a note, the way I had planned, mostly because I figured someday it would be easier to call and explain from far away.

I looked into the mirror and checked my hair. My eyes were tired and burnt from all the speed. There were smudge marks on my cheeks, from the fire, and all that ash, and my hair smelled like wood smoke, and then I turned and saw my mom, standing there.

"Going somewhere?" she said.

My knapsack was packed, behind the door. She looked cross, not yet in control of her destiny, and I knew she'd spend the rest of the day with George in the living room until he finally woke up. Maybe she'd get Mr. Thunder Storm on TV, and I knew I could have told her the truth. I also knew I could have lied. Instead I turned back to the sink and ran some water to rinse my eyes.

"Work," I said.

"When do you get paid?"

"Today. I'll pick up my check today."

She folded her arms and leaned into the doorway. I could see her in the mirror, staring, and she said, "George and I have decided to sell the house. Last night."

The water felt cool and good. It was something I liked, water. I rinsed again and reached for a towel. It was the same towel that had been hanging there for weeks.

"Do you have anything to say?"

"It's your house," I said.

Now she reached for the aloe vera, sitting on a ledge, and handed it to me. "For your sunburn," she said, turning. "Don't be late.

"One more thing," said Mr. Y.

I was in the parking lot, lacing up my boots, and I looked up at him—all fine clothes and dark glasses. The sun was behind him, so I had to squint, and I could feel my sunburn, and the way sometimes your skin begins to itch.

"It's okay," I said, standing. I walked over to him, stood on my toes, and kissed him in the parking lot.

I did it gently, the way you do when you are really grateful.

"No," he said, wiping his mouth. He used the back of his hand. He held me by the arms, and I leaned into him, nudging him, and he said again, "No."

"It's okay," I said. "I understand."

"No, Lacy. You do not."

The truth is, I felt mostly confused—also his penis, which felt more surprised than he did. I held up my arms and said, "One more thing? Things that are never said?"

He laughed now, but gently, in order not to hurt my feelings. He laughed and then he said, putting his arm around me, "The thing about family, real family … The thing about family, Lace, is that there are no conditions. No strings. No payback whatsoever."

"You don't want anything?"

"You are always free to change your mind."

"My mind," I said.

"Yes, Lacy. It's okay to change your mind. A boyfriend, a job. Where you go to school. You don't have to be a lawyer and you are always free to change your mind."

And now he kissed me, on the top of the head, and led me to Rick & Brad's truck. When I slid in, he shut the door for me, as if I were grown up, and he said, "It doesn't mean anything if you know you didn't have a choice."

"Like my dad."

"Your dad didn't have much of a choice. At least not in the end. But you do."

"Okay," I said.

"The soul selects," he said. "Learn to choose."

"Okay."

"Well okay then," he said, nodding. "All you have to do is try hard."

I said thanks, and tried hard not to feel stupid and embarrassed, and he reached through the window and squeezed my shoulder. I was holding on to the steering wheel of Rick & Brad's truck, not crying, and Mr. Y turned away, looking for his car, and his chauffeur, and then he said, "One more thing."

"Okay," I said, sniffling. "One more thing."

"You cannot disappoint me," he said. "Remember that."

I took the aloe vera, too. Later that morning when I stepped into the driveway, the sun was rising in the east, where it was supposed to. I stood in front of my mother's house, which she would soon sell, and held everything I was going to take with me in my arms. It didn't seem like a lot then, standing in the yard: there was a saguaro and a couple bottle trees, and you could see where the weeds were coming up through the ground cover. You could see my friend Mitchell, sitting in his small car, waiting. Then I remembered one more thing and ran inside the house for my disco ball. In the car, I asked Mitchell to keep it safe, in case my mother tried to sell it. We sat in the car for a moment and he asked me if I there was any-place else I had to go. First we went to Rick & Brad's, where I picked up my last paycheck and we all went out for breakfast. We told them about the fire, out past Rawhide, and they said I could have a job with them, anytime, even Mitchell if he ever felt like it, and they told me to say hey to my dad and they went off to work in their boots and Mitchell took me home to his house. His parents were at work, and we went swimming, na-ked in his big pool, and then we took a shower and a nap. In the shower, my hair was still full of smoke, it would take days to wash out completely, and now there was also some chlo-rine, and then I put a lot of lotion on my legs, my shoulders and chest, and Mitchell got out my plane ticket, to check the time, and I fell asleep wrapped up in a towel on his parents' sofa. I don't remember what I dreamed about, but I do remember feeling Mitchell nearby. I remember him rubbing lotion onto my back, rubbing it deeply into my skin, deep circles that make you feel lost, the kind going deep into the center of your spine, and I remember that feeling I had just before he sat on the edge and kissed me on the cheek in order to wake me up. I remember I felt loved, and cold from all the air-conditioning, and very, very scared.

"It's time," he said.

I'd never left home before. And I hoped a little part of me was dying. I hoped it wouldn't be a big part, just the part I'd like to forget: the part about my mother, asking me to cook for George; the part about my dad, and the things he must have done; or my mom, a pencil in her ear, explaining the difference between a lover and a husband, a job and a career, a woman and a man. A man is taught to love himself, and a woman must be taught to love him back, or else she will be lonely, because my mom believed in the healing power of the womb and positive thinking, because my mom believed I could be a star on Broadway, even when I didn't want to. In college, and after, people would ask me about my family, and I would say my father was a former assistant to the governor, before he retired, and I would say my mother was involved with theater, though I wasn't certain just exactly where she was living now, or with whom. I would say *Yes, yes it was a good place to grow up*, particularly when pressed for details I didn't want to give, and I would talk about what it was like, sometimes, going down the river in July, or the smell of mesquite when the rains came in December, the orange blossoms in May and then the long ride through summer all over again. I'd talk about the heat and the way it rose up off the surface like a sunburn. I'd talk about my friend, Mitchell, who wrote me often for the first year, and the pools we used to swim in. I never did mention Mr. Y, because that was part of the bargain, and he continued to pay all of my bills: he offered to send me on to graduate school, though by then I didn't need his help. Twice he visited me in Massachusetts, and we went out to dinner, and he asked me questions about my classes. Once he told me my father had died; he didn't tell me his throat had been slit, in the showers, and that there were no longer any suspects. He didn't tell me there was any more to know because by now I suppose he knew I understood that. And even then there were still new parts forming, especially then, because everything then was still enormous and wide-open: my past, and what I was going to do with my life, and how I was going to live with what I'd done, and whom I was going to love, as opposed to sleep with, or have dinner, in order to someday have my own family. I never heard from Rick & Brad again, which often feels wrong, because they were tall and reminded me of uncles, and because after a while I forgot entirely I had ever slept with Brad a couple times when he was angry with his wife, or she him, because I know now this is precisely the way memory works: you remember what you need to know in order only to remember more. And what you forget is what you never did become. Mostly I remember being seventeen and driving to the airport with my friend, Mitchell Hemly, with whom I had made an oath. He parked his small car in the garage and we walked into the airport full of carpet. All around us there were people going places, and Mitchell bought me peanuts for the long flight ahead, and he took me to the gate because we didn't have any bags to check. At the gate I put my arms around him and didn't cry, and he said *It's Okay Lace* and I said, beginning to cry, *I am not going to change my mind,* and he said *Don't forget to write.* And then some lady in a blue uniform told me it was time to get on board, so I walked through the gateway onto a plane and found my place, beside a window, and never did come home again.

GIVEN

I t began, like most love affairs these days, stupidly enough.
She was twenty-nine and lonely. He was thirty-five and, oh,
you know how they say, in need of release. He was going to
light the world on fire; he liked walks in the moonlight, and
soft rock music by new women artists, and Ravel; he admired
adventurous, eclectic individuals who felt free to release their
inhibitions, as he did, at least according to the advertisement
for himself. I have in fact read a number of these advertisements—the lone one calling out to the other, like wolves lost
upon the plains—for companionship, for company. After the
death of my wife, I recall glancing unabashedly through the
advertisements myself. Sometimes, alone in my bedroom,
drinking a cognac, I could almost get myself fired up, the
way it used to happen, without the excess reading material;
I could get myself fired up and feel what had been lost to me.
Namely, my wife—the woman who taught me to love all wom-
en because, without one, a man, at least a man such as myself, is just a man. As for my wife and I, we named our daughter Annabella, because it was a beautiful name. A beautiful
name for a beautiful blue-eyed girl with a cleft in her chin.
My daughter, my wife's daughter—the sweet, beautiful fruit of
our lives. Annabella.

So when Annabella announced to me last year she was going to marry Adam Petrosky, of Linden, New Jersey (his father
had a foundry there, had sent young Adam off to Rutgers to
study business and communications, a particular area at which
Adam had allegedly prospered), I thought, Well, he sounds like
a decent man from a decent, albeit hardworking, part of town,
which frankly made me think I'd like him. Annabella was, I
knew, lonely, having recently broken up with a boy (and I use
the word judiciously) she had nearly married twice during the
past six years. I supposed like most bright, young women living alone in Manhattan she felt herself at a loss in this world
which, like it or not, does not quite know what to do with a
bright young woman: properly degreed, perfect teeth, a tennis
serve that will spin you dizzy. She spent years of her life on the
courts at the shore when she wasn't off sailing in the bay. This
is what hard work will do for you: it will permit you to provide a blessed life for a perfect daughter in a world uncertain
what to do with her. When you start right out of college making ninety thousand for Chase Manhattan, what's a girl going
to do next? Not everybody, not even my Annabella, wanted to
grow up to become a talking head—a Maria Bartiromo, say, or
a Neal Cavuto? There was only so much room at the top.

Which was Annabella's point entirely: she had seen the top,
albeit from a lower vantage point (and certainly the top in her
mind was neither the NYSE trading floor nor a news desk):
more disturbingly, that's all she saw of it. The top.

Then where? she would ask.

Real power, the sort that makes itself felt, is never public.

And so I could have given her all kinds of answers, because we have been blessed, and because this is what widowed fathers do, I think, after they have provided materially for their daughters. We give our little girls advice. We talk about things like public service and starting up your own software company, perhaps creating a foundation to support chamber music or experimental theater: personally I have always preferred the idea of making money before taking steps to give it away. But we say, we widowed fathers, while pointing out the window, that there is the world, and you are free to make it better. And I could certainly tell Annabella that there were things far more important than worrying about the top. It's the foundation, I would say, upon which all rests; I could tell Annabella all my interesting opinions—glass ceilings or, for that matter, houses. Must the cup always be half empty? I considered telling her about the time last month when our neighbor's husband, Mr. Nishi, drove his Lamborghini with six or seven gears into the swimming pool. Now he walks to the train, apparently too embarrassed to drive down the street. There was a lesson here, I thought, but I could see Annabella tapping her foot impatiently, sipping at her tea, herbal, apple-cinnamon, and I realized stupidly that Annabella of course didn't want my advice. She wanted instead to get laid in the moonlight by a handsome young man who didn't need to shave every day and who also wasn't afraid to reveal his inhibitions, a man who would eagerly give a newborn a bath in a nice, clean porcelain tub, a tub he had picked up at the restoration warehouse himself, and subsequently installed, the very kind of man you see in the advertisements, while she, the lovely Annabella, sat nearby in her cotton pajamas, the buttons discreetly undone, going over the *Wall Street Journal* in her reading glasses. Forget that Annabella with her curly hair and cleft chin had no need for reading glasses. You would think a woman who made her living exchanging the currencies of the Free World would be more likely to grasp the fundamental theatrics of capitalism, but no, you see, because there was simply no reason for Annabella to doubt she could not have what she wanted most. And what she wanted most certainly she deserved—love, from a man who wouldn't put his career first, as I had done; love, from a man who would not neglect his family down the dark and winding middle years after the passion had, like the weather in September, suddenly cooled.

Adam, she told me, that day in the kitchen, warming her hands against her mug of apple-cinnamon tea, tapping her foot. *Of the earth. Remember, Daddy?*

I may have neglected at times my family, but I did teach Sunday school for fifteen years. I knew the roots of our condition. I knew, and felt now daily its absence, the need for somebody you could be permitted to cherish freely and adore, the exquisite desire to receive love and tenderness, the warmth of somebody's toes in bed grazing sleepily against your own. Having been around the block, and a half dozen cities, and then the world, I knew even then Annabella was priming me for something momentous and unexpected, not unlike the time she washed my favorite golf shirt with her purple jeans, or the time she came home from a slumber party, red-eyed and funky-smelling, demanding my position on the legalization of marijuana. She was afraid, you see, that I would disapprove of her young Adam. Of that much I was aware.

So I said bring him out, we'll have dinner at the club, which is where I eat unless I'm feeling lonely. I said, as if she were about to introduce me to a horse, Bring him out and let me have a look.

While I was courting Annabella's mother, my wife, I used to chase her around the Summit Junior High playground in order to bang her head with a book. My math book. I know that men don't always behave as they should.

My wife's father, for example, had been a German industrialist turned state bureaucrat, entirely ruined by the war, and by 1955 he had become a mechanical engineer in New Jersey for General Motors; my wife's mother, who never did speak much English, was a refugee from Milan. Later in high school I would drive Annabella's mother, my soon-to-be wife, out into the countryside with the intention of slipping my hand beneath the fabric of her dress. She was a thin girl with long, yellow hair, her skin honeyed by the summer sun, and then, one day in late August, she merely took it off. Her dress. We were seventeen, standing on a knoll overlooking the entire state of eastern Pennsylvania, and then she turned to me and lifted the summer dress over her head and laid it on the grass as if to make a pallet. It stopped my heart, right there, and which I'll still admit took a while to start working all over again, for when you are looking at a slender girl in the sun with her dress removed in 1956, you are looking at the very work of God. And then, thank God, we married, and she became a professor of

Italian literature, and I have since worked very hard to make certain neither my wife nor daughter ever lacked for anything.

Did I see this coming?

Well, yes, but it's also the nature of surprise to catch us in a flash, in between heartbeats, which doesn't necessarily make you feel any better: you still end up blinking, clutching at your chest. On Thursday I grabbed my nitroglycerin and drove to the club, past Mr. Nishi, who was riding down our street on one of those fold-up bicycles. His balance was a bit shaky, but he waved heartily to me, because we are neighbors and watch each other's houses while the other is on vacation. I believe he has recently invented a chemical compound which is going to make certain forms of cancer obsolete, assuming it works. It has to do with tumors and their ability to clot, or shrink. Mr. Nishi has several children, and his wife, Mrs. Nishi, brought me meals for a week after my wife died.

Among other things I am a thrifty man, which, aside from complementary inflows of tremendous amounts of cash, is how fortunes are made. *Work*, my wife used to say. *Save. Build a little house.* My father-in-law, formerly of Baden Württemberg, had seen his entire fortune destroyed by the war, portions of which I believe Adam Petrosky may have seen reenactments about on the TV. I settled in at the bar, ordered a gin martini, two ounces and extra olives, and watched a little bit of the news regarding the bailout of Long-Term Capital Management, that derelict hedge fund. I thought about hubris, and greed, and that which destroys our ability to reason soundly.

There was a gust of wind, and I heard Annabella's sweet voice, a light and tingly sound like the ringing of bells, talking to the hostess. And here as well, mind you, comes my future son-in-law, the prize stud of the local farm, the swinging dick that's going to blow my socks off. He's wearing, near as I can tell (and I am no expert on these matters), an Italian suit and a Swiss watch—enough fashion easily to buy a decent car or state-subsidized education. His shirt looks like one of those that go nowadays for a full semester's worth of college text-books. I don't know anything about shoes, but you have to give him this—his are very, very shiny. And we are to be eating in the grillroom at the club because the food is (a) the same qual-ity, mediocre, as in the formal dining room and (b) 30 percent less expensive. I am long past needing to talk to anybody I don't want to. I like the bartender in the grillroom, Pierre, who is saving up to buy a tow truck. He dreams of someday owning a fleet of twelve. I do the math briskly in my head because, who knows, maybe someday he'll need a backer. I started out in a bank, 1961. By 1968 Annabella's mother was twenty-seven and pregnant. Sweet. All summer long she swelled up on the lawn behind our wretched two-bedroom apartment, the sprinklers ticking, reading for her comps, and by September Annabella was delivered to us, just like that, and my life became irrec-oncilably bound up with Annabella's own. Summers, while Annabella was still small enough, we would drive around town in a sports car I had rebuilt that kept breaking down. I've known Pierre—and his father, the chief groundskeeper—since Pierre was twelve.

"Yes," Adam Petrosky says to Pierre, nodding condescend-ingly. "Macallan for me. 18 or 25."

He's referring to Scotch, which is what powerful men like to

do on television. Doctor's orders, I am allowed only one martini a day, though I gave those up years ago. Given the celebra-
tory nature of the occasion I say what the hell and ask Pierre
for a Diet Coke. I am at that place in my life where even caf-
feine has become illegal. Annabella takes, as always, the house
Chablis.

At the table, where I order a burger and fries, and Adam
follows suit, as if apologetically, he talks about his own plans.
He is a VP of marketing for Bell Labs just up the street. VP by
thirty-three, he says, proudly. I say that's a fine thing. I think,
listening to him, that he seems to think I want him to be something more than he already is. God's truth, all I want him to
be is decent, honest, and kind. Annabella, meanwhile, is nursing him along, trying to make up for his various and nervous
gaffes. She takes his hand once or twice. She takes my own.

She says, hopefully, "I knew you two would get along."

It's a sad moment for me, a moment I fear marked by some
kind of terrible failure on my part. Because you see I believe Adam Petrosky, for all that fashion and horn-blowing,
is a punk. I believe he is fundamentally dishonest and weak
(though I cannot explain why I believe this, rather I can sense
it, the way when you meet a man you can tell that he sells expensive cars, or derivatives, or that he used to have a drinking problem), and I believe somewhere lurking behind all that
scenery which is the Adam Petrosky who intends to marry my
daughter is a severe case of arrested adolescence, which I read
about once in college. Arrested, as in stopped. The French an-
tecedent is *arrêter,* which means, among other things, to rest. I
say to Annabella, "You are happy?"

She nods, beaming, and replies, "Yes. We want to get married. In December."

"Then I shall have to send you to Greece," I say. I say to Adam, "Or perhaps you would prefer Rome?"

"Haven't thought about it," he says, moodily.

"All roads lead to Rome," I say.

"Mom," says Annabella, discreetly. "She would want us to go to Rome later. With you, Daddy. We could make a trip together."

It is an invitation which displaces immediately my purpose in Annabella's life. And I must flinch, publicly, because Annabella puts her arm around my shoulder as if to comfort me. And now Adam says, rising to shake my hand across the table, as if trying to convince himself, "You won't regret this, sir."

He says this to me, I swear to God, and my heart sinks.

It was a nice wedding. Friends and neighbors, those from the shore, and the club, a few former colleagues and my cardiologist. The Nishis provided the bride and groom with matching bicycle helmets, given the newlyweds' intention to ride bicycles in Greece along the coast. In Greece the water is always beautiful. Annabella wore an ivory dress, the rule these days, and Father Stan provided a ceremony adhering to the traditional liturgy of the Book of Common Prayer. At the proper moment, of course, I gave my daughter away.

They promised to send postcards and drove away to a fine hotel in her mother's Volvo. Shall I describe the moments afterward? I confess I thought about the newlyweds more than

I should have. I thought of Annabella, wearing some fine lace, the kind one sees in the pages of magazines; I thought of her in the arms of her handsome husband; her arms would be shapely, and along the side of her breast would be a fine three-inch scar, barely now detectable, caused by a skating accident when she was nine. Had he even noticed? Of course, and it made me exquisitely sad, that image, and so instead of dwelling on the sexual congress of my now properly wedded daughter, I poured myself a second cognac and took a long, hot bath, watching the snow drift outside my window, while I thought instead about her mother. My wife had been a professor of Italian literature. She had a figure, and a mind, and a navel I could dip my heart into; she had fine, yellow hair and blue eyes, like Annabella, and when she spoke softly I would listen always to her voice: not so much the words she spoke, but the timbre, the music which came always spilling from her throat. What do widowed men do in the bath when they recall their honeymoon? What I did was weep. I lay in the bath and, after a while, as the hot water began to cool, I described the wedding to Annabella's mother. I told my wife about the sweet ivory gown with just the slightest bit of cleavage and the flowers in Annabella's hair and all the bright young friends of hers I hadn't seen in years. I said, as if apologizing, "He's a little arrogant, a tad cocksure for my taste, but we need to respect her judgment."

And then my wife reminded me that her father had not liked me much.

To which I replied, Yes, I know. But your father was a Nazi.

And then he was a Democrat. All fathers are great men, my wife said, which is why their daughters love them.

I told my wife I didn't want to argue. I told her I missed her and that I wished she would come back, and she said, *Yes, I know, Sweet,* and then she said that I shouldn't finish that second cognac on account of my heart. Instead I rose from my bath, put on my robe, and went down to my study where I lit a fire and read late into the night. I remember I was reading Twain, *The Innocents Abroad,* and I remember all the wedding gifts and packages heaped up around the room for safekeeping. Plates, crystal vases. The newlyweds had left behind, among other things, their bicycle helmets.

Meanwhile I didn't think about those helmets for two days. But on Monday, and quite early, I awoke to the sound of the ringing phone. I didn't answer, of course; instead I went downstairs, hopeful for a wrong number, tripping over the bicycle helmets in the den, and a few minutes later the phone began to ring again. It was Adam, apologizing for disturbing me. I stood in the kitchen in my bathrobe and wool socks and considered making a pot of coffee.

"Not at all," I said. "Where are you?"

"Athens," he said. "I'm really very sorry to bother you. Annabella is fine. It's just—"

"You're short of cash," I said.

"Well, it's embarrassing, but that really is the situation. I left behind that envelope in our apartment and, well, you see I've lost my wallet that has my credit cards in it. I don't want Annabella to spend her money."

"What do you need?" I said. I recall I was looking out the window at the birdfeeder. There was an old battle-hardened jay, pecking at some seeds. I gave Adam the phone number of my bank and told him with whom to speak and to leave a routing number and that I would wire him some cash later in the afternoon.

"I really, really—"

"Of course. Not to worry. Give Annabella my love."

"Yes, sir. I will."

He hung up, and I began to worry about their safety, and there was that peculiar delay which takes place sometimes on transatlantic calls, as if sound does actually require just a little bit more time than you'd expect to travel.

Ask me, I know, fathers-in-law can be cold sons of bitches. My own father-in-law, despite his becoming a liberal Democrat, was also once a Nazi—blue-eyed, blond-haired, a jaw made of German steel. He was the kind of man difficult to ignore, especially if one has ever been to Berlin. Knowing my wife's father, and the positions he would take, the drunken arguments he would raise bitterly over sausage and beer, the lesson, it seems to me, is always this: beware the father-in-law, especially if he has once lived on a block destroyed by the ambitions of his own race. So this is what I do after an investigator who sometimes works for me, an Irish guy from Brooklyn who freelances as a lobbyist for the learning disabled … this is what I do after he informs me that my son-in-law has never been employed by Bell Labs. That my son-in-law Adam Petrosky is, rather, a sometimes part-time switchboard operator for New Jersey Cab and Transportation, that he is furthermore some one hundred forty thousand dollars in debt and has two DWIs on his record, as well as a suspended driver's license for failing to pay a dozen parking tickets and that, moreover, he has been evicted from three apartments in the past six years for failure to pay his rent. I am told, wink wink, my son-in-law likes the ponies. And so it is at that moment I decide, first, not to call up the Gaborini brothers in Hoboken and have them break his collarbones, and his kneecaps, and his sternum with a block of ice. I decide, second, not to tell his wife, my daughter, Annabella. And I decide, third, and after several days of calming down, that the guy needs a decent job if he is ever going to care responsibly for himself and his wife and the child she is now carrying. This is what I know, and I carry this information, and these decisions, inside my pocket for close to three months, worrying them each like so much loose change.

Did I see this coming? Well, what if I had? At the wedding his parents mingled with the guests as if constantly surprised that their son was in fact to be married. I had expected more people to arrive on his side of the church, and very few did, which seemed odd given that he wasn't from Utah or the Ozarks. One of Annabella's old boyfriends from high school, a boy who once played the trumpet and who now presides over a publicly held Internet retailer, seemed openly hostile to Adam. Niggling things, all in all, and inconsequential in and of themselves. It was the purchase of their house in Westfield that got me going—the solid lump sum in cash from Annabella's trust. What, I thought, he doesn't have a salary?

Weeks later, after my discovery by way of my Brooklyn PI, I was sitting in the den on a Monday afternoon, which is sadly what retired widowers often do, watching Lifetime—Television for Women. It's the kind of programming my wife would have scoffed at. The day's afternoon movie, however, had me fairly riveted, wherein a woman falls in love with a married man who fakes his death so he can leave his faithful wife and two children and join up with the New Woman, whom he subsequently marries. His background is very shady, and hush hush, because he is a top secret military specialist who blows things up in Guam and Libya and the like. Consequently, he convinces New Woman and her family that he cannot whisper a word about his past. You see where this is going. After he fakes his death, a bicycle-riding accident, he obviously can't return to his top secret military hoodoo special ops troop, and so to earn a living he starts fixing up and selling houses, but that doesn't work so well, given that he's used to killing targets, as opposed to selling them, and eventually he begins to apply his Navy Seal tactics to robbing banks. Keep in mind much of this action-romantic-drama is interspersed with commercials for tampons and bathroom cleaners—for the target audience, apparently, and here I am, nibbling on pretzels and watching the strong, virtuous New Woman sleuth about as she makes her discoveries. She is victorious, of course, and not a *victim*, because this is Lifetime—Television for Women, and sitting there I understand perfectly well that my pregnant daughter, Annabella, is sitting at home on her new couch watching the very same program.

I called her up, and she answered quickly, sniffling. "Oh hi, Daddy," she said. "I was just watching this awful movie."

"The one about the Navy Seal whose hands are made of death?"

"You watch Lifetime?" she said, giggling, albeit nervously.

And then I invited her and Adam over for Sunday. We could watch a game, or make spaghetti—play cards, maybe, and pick out names for the baby. Before Annabella hung up, she said to me, still a little bit in shock, "That woman sure was duped."

"It's a movie," I said, hopeful to cheer her up. "Happens all the time."

And then, on the appointed day, I put on my best cardigan and loafers, and at the given hour my daughter and son-in-law arrived one fair Sunday afternoon upon my doorstep.

Football weather, which reminds me of girls in long socks and scratchy sweaters and bullies who used to beat me up after school. By now Annabella is six months pregnant, living quite pleasantly at home, decorating—bored out of her gourd. Adam has recently been promoted again at Bell Labs, where he reports now only to the CFO. Even Annabella does not quite believe this, but she lets it go. One wonders just what she does know. Meanwhile she pats her swollen tummy, reclines gingerly on the couch and asks me to fetch her some sherbet. Maybe a glass of mineral water? It's an old family joke we have: the one who thinks up the treats first is the one who does not have to fetch them.

Adam stands and offers to get the snacks. He is eager, it seems, not to be alone with me.

"Lime?" Adam asks. "Orange?"

After he leaves the room, I say, reaching into my pocket, "He seems to be doing fine. This new promotion?"

She leans forward, bursts into tears, and says, "Oh, Daddy. He's been fired. Management reshuffle, they said, and he's just too proud to tell you. I told him it was no big deal."

"I see."

"We're okay," she says. "I mean the house is in my name. But his car payments on the Porsche are going to kill our liquidity."

Always the investment banker, my daughter. "Sell it," I say. "Cut your losses."

"That would mean failure," she says, biting her lip. "I told him he should have bought a Volkswagen, that you would like him more, but of course he didn't listen. He thought it would impress you."

"Hey," Adam calls from the kitchen. "What time's the game on?"

I speak, quickly, because this is important. "What else do you know?"

She nods, wipes her nose on her sleeve. Someday she is going to have a child that is going to belong to me, however indirectly. She says, "I know he lies. About stupid things, like whether or not he played football in high school. Stupid. And I know he has a lot of bills."

"And?"

"I know if I divorce him I will be the laughingstock of this town."

I say very carefully, so she will not question my intent, "That is not a reason to stay married to him. We've never cared too much about this town, anyway—"

"It's a reason," she says, firmly, "if I can fix him."

"Annabella," I say. "I will do whatever you want me to. I know a software firm that's looking for a sales rep. We could get him in fairly easily. All he has to do is know how to sell. We know he can do that."

She takes the insult to herself well, as I have obviously intended it. Stupid, I tell myself, insulting your daughter. "Sorry," I say.

She says to me, glancing up, "I am not stupid, Daddy." And then, "Can you have *them* call?"

"Of course."

Adam returns, ice cream bowls in his arms, a bag of chips. He brings me a beer, to go along with his own, even though he should know by now that I do not drink beer. He says, "I sure am glad we came over. This is a great day for a game." He looks at Annabella and says, "You crying again?"

"Hormones," she says, evidently tweaked. She rises from the couch, clumsily, and says, "You forgot my mineral water." She says, beginning to laugh, "Daddy, there are some things you just can't fix."

Adam laughs, *heh heh heh*, thinking this is one of those typical women's lib jokes against lazy husbands. I, however, know better, because I know and love my daughter more than she can imagine possible, at least more than she can imagine until her own child is delivered, and so I watch Adam watch the television, though it is not yet turned on. I watch my daughter leave the long, wide room, waddling the way her mother once did while pregnant: years ago, my daughter was nothing more than the gathering of flesh and nerves inside the belly of my wife. And this is what I think, albeit a little cruelly. I think a son-in-law should never, never go to a strip joint with his father-in-law, though I am certain if I invited Adam he would attend. Certainly I think a son-in-law should always bring mineral water to his wife when she is pregnant, no matter how bitchy she might be. And I think it's finally about time I had a talk with Adam Petrosky out behind the barn.

"Hey," I say. "I need to run out to the country and was hoping you'd come along. There's some property up there a friend says might be worth developing."

His eyes light up at this. Property, development. He says, "You won't miss the game?"

Anybody who knows me knows I hate professional sports almost as much as I hate liars.

Spectacle, it no longer attracts.

"Nah," I say, tossing him the keys to my car. "You drive?"

The lesson of World War II, the war in which my father died in Italy, is this: if you give away things which don't belong to you, like Poland, or France, then you are someday going to have to take them back.

I was neither a perfect man nor husband. And the most difficult thing for me now, being a widower, is knowing that I have no longer any secrets from my wife. She is a ghost, and ghosts know all, especially when you tell them everything, anyway. It's not as if I am about to fib to the spirit of my dead wife. And it's not as if God isn't going to tell her the truth, anyway, or Saint Peter, up there making notes upon his ledger. And the secrets in my life are generally speaking not bad—I have never killed anyone, or acted out of mean-spiritedness in any consequential manner—but the things I *have* done, the awful things, are certainly and irrevocably shameful. Like the time in Santiago when I stumbled out of a brothel without my wallet—trust me, businessmen abroad are always, always in mortal peril, so much so that my wife had to cancel my credit cards from the States. These specific incidents seemed to recur on a ten-year cycle, and after I turned fifty, I swore by God that this time I would behave, and given that the sap wasn't as pressing then as it had been in my younger years, I was able to be virtuous (though the victory remains fraught with complication, for if one is not tempted, then where is the joy in overcoming that temptation?). I know, for example, that I never once considered having an affair with anybody because I simply could not imagine the enormous legwork and deceit therein—and with whom would I dally, anyway? My secretary? A twenty-year-old I met in a fern bar? But the truth is a man who has an affair, however stupidly, is at least following some basic understanding of commitment—serial monogamy, at least, is better than *no* monogamy. It's better than plain, gravid lechery. And although I told my wife about each of these awful incidents, not always right away, and although I do believe she has in fact forgiven me for them, I have never quite been able to tell her just *why* they happened. To be sure, the reasons varied, depending upon the season. Sometimes, I was lonely. Other times, I was drunk on red, red wine *because* I was lonely. I know in Rome I was frustrated with losing what I saw everybody having on the television: the endless, nameless thrill of seduction, week after week; the sheer ecstasy of being won over by a beautiful woman whose name is foreign on the tongue. I had a married colleague who used to brag about his moose in Taiwan: I knew married men who kept women in London, and Singapore. Venice. The middle road of marriage is awkward for men (which is not to say it's easy for their wives) because it's hard to remember just where you thought you were heading: all around you are things you will never have again, like unblemished skin, and good health: like the possibility of being seduced. Eventually, and to protect myself, as well as my family, I gave up on most television and returned to Dickens, and Mann, and blessed of saints, Tolstoy. But in Santiago, when I walked into Madam Lazar's shortly after turning forty-three, I know perfectly well I was itching for an excuse to get a divorce and buy a sports car and hire a personal trainer in order to build me some pectorals. Not long afterward I had to call my wife collect, to explain about the credit cards, and the fact I would be needing twelve stitches in the back of my head assuming I could find a doctor famil- iar with antiseptic; I had awakened, you see, in the gutter of a slum, having pissed my pants: there were children with dirty faces who should have been on their way to school, had there been a school, pointing at me and laughing. Apparently I had fallen there several hours earlier.

I remember my wife wanting to know which suit it was I had been wearing that morning in the gutter, as if this detail might make for her the sin more negotiable. Trust me, it's not easy being good, especially if you are married to a woman who never does anything wrong. I'm not talking about the little things, like forgetting to take the dry cleaning for seventeen months until it's all covered with mold in the basement. Or a stolen kiss with an equally tipsy colleague at a Christmas party. I mean, is that all you have to complain about? You take my point. Meanwhile my wife raised our daughter and taught her classes at the university and forgave me when I needed her forgiveness more than bread, or water, to survive the very day after. What I am saying is my wife did and continues now to sustain me, and she most certainly did not watch Television for Women. When I had my first heart attack, she held my hand in the hospital and promised me, then and for all time, that I was not as bad a man I always feared I was. She knew, you see, my gravest frailties, my deepest flaw—vanity.

So.

So this is the catalogue of personal shame I am rifling through while Adam Petrosky drives us up into the state of New York. Eventually the traffic begins to thin and we are aiming for a small farming town near Poughkeepsie. The town is now the home of a new prison, the type for serial killers and rapists. At the old prison, the good prisoners, as opposed to the ineducable, are permitted to work the local farm. We take the thin roads, Adam evidently chewing on some thoughts of his own, and I say after a while, eager to give him a bit of rope, "It's not easy when your wife is pregnant. It's as if they disappear from you."

"Pardon?"

"Annabella. Being pregnant. It's a hard thing for a husband, too."

"Actually," he says, "it's been a breeze."

That ends that line, at least for another twenty minutes. I tell him which roads to take. I explain that the farm belongs to a friend of mine who doesn't know what to do with it. The property taxes are eating him up. He can't find anybody to work it. Dairy farming just doesn't bring in what it used to. Apparently, the world has too much milk.

I say, pointing to a field, "When I was a kid, I used to work on this farm. Used to plow that very field."

"Uh huh."

"You ever do any farm work?"

"Oh sure," he says. "Lots of it. I worked on a ranch in Texas for two years."

"While you were in college?"

"What?"

"You worked on a ranch while you were in college?"

"Yeah. I mean right after."

I remind myself of a fundamental condition given to all liars. Whenever they are about to lie, they always ask you to repeat the question, which gives the liar time to calculate his or her response. It's the kind of symptom I used to fire people for, no questions asked. Lying.

For a while we drive around the fields, and I speculate about what it would take to lay sewers and roads. I'm wondering if Adam might be a little interested. I could go in with him if I trusted him. It's a stupid idea, of course.

Stupid, so we go into town for coffee, and later on the way out, heading home, past the razor wire for all the convicts, I ask him if he'd like to visit a horse farm.

"Sure," he says, brightening up.

"These are racers. Or Arabians. Heck, I don't know."

I tell him to pull off onto a road, and we drive up to a large,

recently painted barn. We step outside. The fields are gor-
geous, even in fall, marked with whitewashed board fences.
Now a woman in waders and overalls greets us. "I was just
wondering," I call, "if I could show my son-in-law around. He
likes the ponies."

He doesn't flinch, the poor soul. The woman appears to
recognize me, though she does not appear certain. Still, you
never know, we might be a couple of potential investors. She
ambles over, takes us into the barn, proudly, eager for a chance
to show off her work. Before entering, she turns and points to
a large black stallion. As in enormous. "That's Sir Galahad of
Green Stream," she says, pointing, while sliding open an enormous door. "And this is his castle."

Sir Galahad isn't much interested. We step inside the barn,
which is clean as a whistle, the kind which will pierce your
eardrums. And she gives us the tour. Here is where they store
the oats. And there is the breeding room. And in there, the
phantom. The phantom, I know, is similar to the type of horse
malnourished teenage gymnasts use on television networks
during the Olympics. Only this type is for teasing the stud,
getting him to mount, while the handlers begin whanging
away at the stud while a teaser mare lifts her tail in front of
him until he ejaculates into a condom the size of a Hefty bag.
The condoms, apparently, are hand-sewn for each stud. The
semen sells for thousands an ounce. Inside the lab, the woman
shows us a rack of condoms, each about two feet long, with the
name of its owner just beneath.

"That," says the woman, beaming, "is where the rubber
hits the road, so to speak."

She shows us more things, pictures and the like. She wants to know if she can have the general manager give us a call some time. She uses the word *shelter* often, by which she is not referring to rooftops. Eventually we wave good-bye, pleasantly, and she tells me to come by any time, and Adam, too, and now we walk out into the cool fall air. It is going to snow soon, I can feel it in my bones. I am not going to be around forever.

Adam rushes to the car, but I stroll over to the fence. I reach out for Sir Galahad and pat him on the head. He's a ferocious animal, the kind who'd win a war, the kind who'd mount a mare or piece of gymnasium equipment with equal abandon. Do we control the species because the species cannot control itself? Adam strolls up, eager to leave, shivering, and I think now is as good a time as ever.

"Given," I say, "Annabella can be a bitch. She is headstrong and smart and that makes her sometimes difficult."

"Not really—"

I say, "You are a pathological liar."

This gives him pause. He says, "What?"

"We can also assume Annabella is the most important person in my life."

"I don't know what you're getting at," he says. "I don't—"

"You can come clean and get a job and pay your bills," I say. "I can help you do that. Or you can get a divorce."

He says nothing.

"A sin is not a life," I say. "Not if you look it in the eye."

"Uh huh."

That's the real problem, of course. Even if Adam could begin to behave, he'd have to spend the rest of his life in our family knowing it wasn't secret. It's why marriages fall apart, I'm thinking. *Pride.* Most things are forgivable—I ought to know—but the atoning for the sin hurts nothing in comparison to the other knowing you have committed it. I say to Adam, "To live with someone you've hurt deeply requires sacrifice. It's always going to be easier to walk away."

"I have done nothing wrong," he says. "And I resent being called a liar."

We make our choices, don't we? All of life is a test—an opportunity for us to show our mettle. Before parting, a man can say to another either *stay in touch* or *good luck.*

"Okay," I say, nodding. "Okay. Just so we are clear, I would prefer the divorce. Regardless of who asks for the divorce, I will expect you to forswear all rights to the baby. And if you fight it, I will bury you in court. Adam, I will spend you into the grave, and then I will come to collect. But in exchange for a peaceful settlement, the kind in which you politely disappear from our lives, I will see to it that you are not completely abandoned. A tidy sum, to be delivered annually for three years. Think of it as an allowance."

The corners of his mouth begin to rise. He says, catching himself, "I love Annabella, you don't know what you are asking."

"Adam," I say, "I don't ask. I am presenting you with two choices. If you tell Annabella about this conversation, the deal is off." I say, heading for the car, because I now actually intend to drive, "It's up to you."

Later, after I drop him off at Annabella's house, I say, "Good luck."

There is one secret which I have never even told my wife, and if she is to know then she will have to go directly to the source. When her father died, the former Nazi, my father-in-law, I cleaned out his garage, and in so doing I found his stash of propaganda and pornography. Dirty little films, with animals; recently manufactured flags of the swastika. Various leaflets and brochures from the KKK and the like. The propaganda did not surprise me necessarily, and the pornography seemed to me essentially harmless, but the secret—and this is the part about which I am so utterly ashamed—the secret is that I was glad. I was glad the old Nazi had been a pervert to boot.

I never told my wife what I had found. And knowing what I know about Adam, it's obvious he doesn't have a choice—he's going to take the cash. Maybe not right away, but where the soil is fertile, the roots grow deep, and soon I will be free of him, and in being free of him, I will have removed from him the possibility of raising his own child. This is another secret I intend to keep.

Another day, another month. Soon it will be Christmas, and yesterday, while working on the driveway, Mr. Nishi lost control of his snow blower, which attacked the large elm by our garage. There are chunks missing from it the size of bowling shoes.

Don't ask, they say. Mm hmm.

Annabella hasn't spoken to me about her forthcoming di-

vorce, but I know it's coming, the same way a man knows he
will soon take a drink, or a cigarette, long after he has given up
that sort of thing. Most recently, Annabella's car has been im-
pounded. Apparently, Adam started using it after he lost the
Porsche. Porsches are made in Stuttgart, where my father-in-
law once owned a factory that supplied the Wehrmacht with
tank treads and turrets. The finest car in the world. Meanwhile
Adam ran up another dozen parking tickets and this morning
Annabella went to pick up her car from the lot in Newark.
She stood there in line, eight months pregnant, for two and a
half hours; the heat in the building was blasting, its furnace
out of whack. When she finally reached a clerk, a woman with
gold teeth recently empowered by the State of New Jersey to
demand fees from delinquent parking-ticket-violators, the
woman refused to take a check for the seven-dollar adminis-
trative portion of the bill. That is, Annabella wrote out a check
for nine hundred dollars to pay her husband's fine, but to file
the paperwork in order to acknowledge that she had paid the
fine, she was required to pay the seven-dollar fee in cash, and
naturally she had no cash. Who does anymore? So the woman scolded her, my Annabella, while Annabella asked why her
check for seven dollars wasn't good enough. Two separate kit-
ties, apparently, and the woman began to raise her voice at
my pregnant daughter. It is then that she started crying, my
daughter, which I know from experience is when she becomes
most resilient. Runs in the genes, this resiliency. So she turned
around and asked the people behind her in line if anybody
would give her seven dollars for a check for fourteen—a 100

percent return—but of course nobody is going to accept a personal check from a pregnant lady with tears on her face in a New Jersey state office for violators of the law.

"Look," Annabella said to the woman, the bureaucrat behind the glass. "Please. Take my check. I'll make it out to you. You have lunch money?"

"Wouldn't be fair," said the woman. "You should have known better."

And that is when, while being properly bludgeoned by an employee of the state, that is when (I am certain of it) Annabella decided she would divorce Adam Petrosky. Not a thing she was going to ask. She would do it next week, after she spoke with a real estate agent, after she checked with me about coming home just for a few months until she collected her wits. She would test the idea gently, like a parent delivering a ransom, to gauge my response.

And she would come back home, and we would read together in the den and eat ice cream, and sometimes I would look up at Annabella from my book or ice cream and remember the particular girl she came from. Sometimes she would turn to me and say, out of the blue, *You should have known better,* and we would laugh until it was no longer funny, only sad and tender, like an elbow you've knocked against the doorknob. And then Annabella would return to her book, and I would return to mine, and I would think again about that particular girl she came from. And I would remember how after Annabella was born I watched, awestruck and utterly terrified, her mother give Annabella her breast. It was that very sight, the sight of my infant daughter taking her mother's breast, which made me understand then and for all time that no man alive will ever be capable of such an act of mercy and tenderness and exquisite faith. Dear God, the saying goes, bless this life. *Bless this life.* And then the life prospered, in and of itself, and Annabella grew up and dated boys and smoked marijuana and I sent her by God to the finest college money could buy, and my wife and I lived our lives and waved good-bye to our daughter until my wife was diagnosed with breast cancer. For a while we were hopeful, all together, and sometimes the Nishis joined us for meals during the sleepy periods of chemotherapy, and after the hopefulness turned to something more realistically bitter, my wife died on a Sunday morning shortly after the azaleas bloomed. Just before we were alone, in the bedroom, and I remember she asked me to pull back the blinds. There were birds singing, and she talked about a time we spent in Naples, and the old gardener who always brought us cocoa, the rich Italian kind laced with cream, and she died, and I closed her eyelids, and Annabella arrived an hour later. After a few days, Annabella cleaned out her mother's closet, and her mother's office at the university. Annabella ordered flowers to be delivered monthly to the house. And next month, when Annabella goes into labor, I will take her into delivery, where we will wait nervously for her doctor, a sweet Pakistani with two kids of her own, and I will be holding Annabella's hand while the water begins spilling out of my daughter's body in preparation for the life which is to follow. I will be listening for the sound of its cry.

As for me? I am a fallen man with a weak heart. But I know that the Lord giveth and the Lord taketh away.

Here, the doctor will say, handing me the shears to cut the cord. *It's time.*

And then there will be another life to raise.

LIFE IN THE BODY

My father is a strong man. But in October of 1962, I imagine he is uncertain of his depths. Winter is decidedly in the air, and Khrushchev is in the process of installing missiles in Cuba—a twelve-minute burn to Miami, a few minutes more to Washington. Driving out of the city of Chicago, heading for home along with half a million others, my father is worried mostly about the future.

Certainly he does not know that I am soon to be conceived. Right now the traffic is heavy and slow. The sky, early winter, is absent of relief: in the Rust Belt one learns to spot the symptoms early, and through his windshield my father looks up at the sky—the color of manufactured steel, solid as a door. On the seat beside him rests his briefcase. It is a briefcase that my mother picked out, as a wedding gift, and inside the case among his pencils and slide rule and new life insurance policy lies the hope of his future at Maryvale. Maryvale has its fingers in washing machines and machine guns, though it is known mostly for its influence upon automotive exhaust—tailpipes, mufflers; twelve years from now my father will design a prototype catalytic converter specifically for Ford. But right now he is a new recruit, a recent acquisition of a corporate takeover, and he knows little of exhaust.

My father, after being released from the Korean conflict, during which he repaired a network of IBM computers inside a tall Manhattan building, returned to Goodyear, where he worked with a team that developed airplane tires. He skipped around for the next several years: Firestone, and tubeless tires; Bendix, where he worked on brakes; Studebaker, where he flirted with overall design on the Avanti project; and later Ford, where he was responsible for coming up with the suspension for the Lincoln Continental—then still just a fine idea. The long hood wasn't yet under consideration, but it was at Lincoln that he found his direction, his place in the automotive world of manufacturing and design: he would be a specialist, and he would specialize in suspension. So my father settled in Cleveland and took on a job at Roman, as in Roman Shock Absorbers. Roman also makes leaf springs and U-joints, but Roman will soon be bought out by Maryvale, the company that also has its thumbs in machine guns and washing machines. In the spirit of increasing shareholder value, Maryvale is extending its reach within the automotive industry; they send a team of gray suits to Cleveland, have a look around, smoke a lot of cigarettes. They buy the company outright and fire everybody on the design team except my father. Afterward they tell my still-standing father he needs his own office. They tell my father to buy a couple suits, to take a few days off. They tell my father to take the little wife and to go look for a nice house in Chicago.

-20-

Time runs fast and out, like water from a pot, into the very heart of the matter. Down, says a man who fights. *Down for the count.*

The little wife is five foot even, raven-hearted with two kids of her own and coal black hair down to her waist. She has no chin to speak of, but as my father likes to point out, her struts are fine and true. She was raised an orphan in a Catholic convent north of Dodge City, Kansas. Consequently, she believes in God. She is also convinced my father is sleeping with his new secretary in Chicago—a woman named, of all things, Eve.

And because she is convinced my father is sleeping with Eve, my mother is very, very angry. Right now, aside from being decidedly fertile, she is putting my older brother down for his nap. The bedspread is blue, and Connor, who doesn't want to take a nap, is crying fitfully. He takes a small fist and punches my mother on the cheek.

"No," she says. "Mommy has to talk. Connor has to sleep."

"No," Connor wails. "No."

"Daddy will be home and you can play. With Daddy."

"He's not my daddy."

When my mother slaps Connor, he quiets down. She is, in fact, proud of her slap—her fine hand and slender fingers, neatly collected, a skill several nuns taught her as a child. It was the nuns in that convent who also taught her how to spy—going through people's pockets, their wastebaskets, the wallet and the purse. In the kitchen, sitting at the table over his fourth glass of wine, mopes Father Tim, who is waiting for Connor to settle down and for my mother to return.

And my mother, standing in the doorway, having a last look at Connor—his cheek tear-stained and pink—does my mother really want to do this? Quite frankly, she hates Chicago—the cement and factories, the constant spread of industrial incorporation. When she married my father, in a distant, wooded Ohio suburb, they moved into a log cabin. The cabin had a loft, and my father made furniture at night; he played with Connor and taught him how to hold a saw. *Look*, my father would say. Later my father took Connor and Maureen into a city courtroom and changed their name. "From now on," my father said to Connor, holding his hand, "you're a McGowan. Just like me."

Connor has yellow hair, unlike my father. Connor's real father was on the skids—strung out somewhere in San Francisco. My mother had once said she loved him, that she was pregnant; that sex was one kind of sin, abortion entirely another. She had called up my father on the telephone from South Bend, Indiana, where she worked in a small radio station, writing ad copy, and she said to my father, "Mac, I'm going to marry him."

"Well," my father said. "Good luck."

Three years later, she was back on the telephone with a two-year-old and an infant. My father was working at Studebaker. He bought things for my mother like milk and chocolate and shoes. For Christmas, he gave her a sweater, the same style he gave to a woman he was dating, only he mixed up the packages. My mother opened her sweater, which was *Large,* and said my father had some explaining to do. That night they must have talked a lot, particularly in bed. In college, my father once went flying through a second-story window—bathtub gin—and she had nursed his wounds: a broken ankle; a long, deep cut along his chin; she had seen him naked often, despite the wounds. And I imagine that Christmas, with Connor tucked into bed, dreaming of someday having his own dad, I imagine that my mother knew exactly what she was doing then. My father was tall, profoundly shy unless drunk, and dressed terribly. He wore his hair short to keep it out of his eyes. His fingernails were full of axle grease and smelled like gasoline and nicotine. His arms were hard as galvanized steel, and he dated a tall woman who required large, plush sweaters, and he liked to work. Nights, when the light was gone, he drank beer and looked at the sky.

"You should marry me, Mac."

"Not hardly."

My mother laughed dishonestly. In bed she punched him with her fist. My father was tired, cranky from having put together a tricycle for Connor and Maureen, out in the garage, which was cold. He was tired of hanging out with a woman and her kids without having a specific reason. He liked reasons. He needed to understand how the pieces fit together, in order to make a machine, or a common understanding.

"I'm getting too old," my mother said. "Connor's growing up. He needs a dad."

"You should take that job," my father said. "More money. More men."

My mother had a job offer from an advertising agency

in Michigan that handled accounts for General Motors. Apparently, somebody had decided they needed a woman's point of view, even if nobody there had any particular intention of using it.

"You're calling me a whore?"

"Jesus, Linda. I'm calling you a modern woman."

"But not modern enough, eh?"

At this, my father rolled over onto his side. He shut his eyes, because he was tired, and because he wanted to get some sleep. He thought about the way my mother's hair fell against his back.

"Mac? I can't keep doing this."

"Maybe I should leave, then."

And then my mother stretched across his back to find the light.

−19−

She took the job in Michigan. Then her husband looked her up, caught a bus, and pissed on Connor and beat him senseless. My father was in Minnesota, doing cold-weather testing for Firestone. He drove to Detroit and said enough was enough.

I know only the man's name. Goose. He too was a Catholic from Dodge City. His family—the Goose Shoe Store chain—had a moderate amount of money and wanted him to find a wife. A wife, it was believed, could keep a moderately wealthy man from drink, as well as provide an heir. When Maureen was born, Goose stole my mother's gasoline credit card and robbed a liquor store in Topeka. Then the family cut him off and asked my mother to move out of town.

It happened long before I was born—Connor, and Maureen. Connor has yellow hair, a crew cut, because my father likes it that way, and right now Connor is trying to lie in bed and listen to the dusk. He can see light creeping through the gingham drapes. It's a small house, a South Chicago bungalow, newly built like the dozen others on the same block. My parents have rented this house while my father saves for a down payment on one my mother plans to pick out soon. A suburb, someplace with a lawn. In the meantime, my mother no longer works, and Connor doesn't want to take a nap. He will soon turn five, he hasn't had a nap in months, and if Father Tim stays for supper, then Connor will not have to talk to his new dad. Connor is still mad at my father for making him eat his peas.

So Connor lies in bed, racing, because that's what his brain does. It races. He goes around inside his head like a track. In winter, when he is expected to sit still, he often breaks his toys, and after a while, he begins to bang his head against the wall. His forehead, there where it won't hurt as much, but just enough for him to feel good. If it doesn't hurt, he won't have a reason to be crying, which he does, silently. After a while, he remembers to keep count, and then he loses it.

—18—

My father feels uncomfortable in a suit. To save money, he bought himself two, each the same, and several white shirts. It helps to think of it as a uniform, and on the radio of his '53 Ford, the second '53 Ford he has owned, each engine rebuilt by himself … my father listens to the news. The traffic is deadlocked now. People in thick clothes are trying to build a freeway ramp, but they haven't had much practice yet, and meanwhile the southbound traffic has been shifted into a single, frozen lane. And the news is particularly grim. Kennedy has ordered a blockade of Soviet ships steaming into Cuba. He has made clear his willingness to fire on those ships that are bringing to Cuba equipment that will make the missiles operable. Khrushchev has said Kennedy has missiles in Turkey. It is only right that he, The Big Nikita, protect Cuba. Khrushchev mentions often and with remarkable derision the incident at the Bay of Pigs.

My father doesn't know that Dean Acheson has already urged the president to fire on Cuba. Once the Soviet missiles in Cuba become hot, the entire nation is at risk. And Kennedy, stretching the small of his back, insists there must be some alternative. McNamara, secretary of defense, argues that a missile is a missile, that a missile in Cuba pointed at Detroit is no different than a missile in Moscow pointed at Detroit. On this matter, apparently, McNamara is a *dove*, and not a *hawk*, and Bobby Kennedy, who is merely the president's brother, prefers a naval blockade—like a *duck*, Acheson thinks. Consequently, Acheson is dispatched to Paris, to apprise de Gaulle, while Kennedy makes a seventeen-minute speech, declaring his intent to respond militarily—which means B-52s over Moscow, and Soviet IL-28 bombers over St. Louis; which means lighting up those Jupiter missiles in Turkey, even if they are obsolete, because this means global thermonuclear war. And as my father listens to the news, sitting in traffic, the signal begins to drift. The announcer's voice begins to fade, and my father hits the dash of his '53 Ford once, then twice, and looks up into the sky.

On the seat beside him in his briefcase lies a sketch. The sketch is of a shock absorber, one to be controlled by air. He has no idea how to make the valves seal, but a shock absorber that is flexible to the needs of the nuclear family—one that can accommodate both light and heavy loads—will revolutionize the entire industry. It is an industry that services automobile manufacturers, which in turn service the needs of a consumer-driven economy, which my father believes must inevitably lead to war. In this life, there simply isn't room enough for everybody to be rich.

Khrushchev knows this, and so he plans to take now what he wants before the United States can buy it. By making a feint at Cuba, Khrushchev intends to dig his Soviet heels further into Europe—namely, Berlin. Meanwhile Kennedy invokes the Monroe Doctrine and considers, once again, invading Cuba. He rocks in his chair while my father, stuck in traffic, worries about the seal. Everything, my father knows, must rest upon the quality of the seal.

−17−

Father Tim is in love with my mother, always has been. In Kansas, Father Tim wasn't yet a priest; he was a kid, a Protestant who went to the Catholic high school, and took my mother to all the dances. Tim is two years younger than Goose, that man somewhere now in San Francisco, strung out, and Tim is also married. He has two kids of his own. He is an assistant rector at the local Episcopal church. When he scratches at his beard, prematurely gray, he really does appear to be uncomfortable.

At church, dressed in a gray suit, my father listens patiently to Father Tim's sermons. My mother loves to dance, although she is now married to a man who dresses horribly. She married my father in a courtroom to avoid formality and a wedding band—the kind that plays music badly and insists on everybody dancing. My father doesn't wear a ring.

And my mother knows the rules that govern this world. She knows that old lovers always sleep together, no matter how hard they may try not to: intimacy, once formed, longs always to return to its origins. That first, initial spark. She knows too that God prefers shame to anger—that once angry, one no longer has the possibility for remorse, until that anger has long since passed. My mother wants to be close to God, as well as the men she loves, and my mother wants to feel ashamed, if only because it speeds up the process of forgiveness—divine and absolutely necessary for this life.

Having lost one man already, my mother does not intend to lose another.

At the wedding, which took place in a courtroom, my father gave my mother a ring that had been brought over to America on a boat. It belonged to his grandmother, my father said. My father said, "Aside from my tools, it's the only decent thing I own."

−16−

Does Eve really believe she is in love with my father? Eve is a young woman, nearly liberated, living in a city two-flat near the North Side, though still not yet far enough north to be expensive or fully liberated. On her desk, beside her typewriter, stand a lot of books. She dreams someday of being an executive secretary and taking frequent trips to Honolulu. Sometimes, in my father's office, on her knees, maybe, or stroking his face, she dreams that he will take her there.

"No commitments," Eve says, hopefully. "No strings."

Like most practical men, my father distrusts suspense and its false promise for resolution. Instead my father believes that when one person contemplates adultery, then so too does that person's mate. It's something one finds in the air, floating by— innuendo, and surprise. He imagines for a moment his wife, Linda, in bed with another man. My father imagines his adopted children, Connor and Maureen, watching him through the window. It makes him angry, this matter of precise and living fact: Connor, and Maureen. To be a kind and loving father, he shall need always to be in control. What my father wants most in this life is a son of his own making.

"You need another boss," my father says to Eve.

"You're firing me?"

"No," says my father. "But if we are going to continue like this, then you cannot work for me."

"Oh."

"Otherwise," my father says, "otherwise, you can still work for me, and we can call this off."

Secretly, my father wants to call it off. He likes his office and his new appointment and previously uncomplicated mornings. He only slept with Eve in an effort to convince himself he should divorce his wife. Eve is a sweet girl, but if he stays with her, she will wind up telling him what to do. My father is most afraid of being told just what to do, especially by a woman.

He runs his hand across her breast. He traces a vein, and with the winter light falling into his office, Eve's body shimmers in the dusk. She has goose pimples. From the cold, my father reasons. He is not going to remove his tie.

"You don't wear a ring," Eve says. "Why not?"

My father laughs, and looks at his hand, which is scarred from years of use. "Currents," he says, laughing. "I can't stand being shocked."

—15—

Birds fly, missiles fly. Where is my sister?

At the age of seven, Maureen is already far ahead of her time. Having skipped one grade, her teachers urge that she skip another. Wednesdays, after school, she reads books to kids in kindergarten. It makes her feel old, like a teacher or a tree.

Maureen does not yet know precisely where books come from. She imagines a room full of old men, each leaning heavily on a desk, writing very carefully. She knows the men are old because it must have taken years and years of practice to make each letter perfect. She is just learning cursive herself and has particular trouble with her *S*'s. When she turns the page, after reading about a dog named Spot, and a boy named Dick, she decides she'd like to have a dog, too—one she wouldn't dream of naming Spot, because that name has already been taken.

She is reading to a boy named Toby Cameron, though she only pays attention to his first name. He is a slow, thick boy who often gets lost on his way to the lunchroom. His parents are pleased that Maureen will read to him, and in return offer to keep her until five o'clock, when my mother drives to Toby's house and picks her up in the baby blue Volkswagen. My father wants to sell the Volkswagen because the engine is in the back. Maureen doesn't know what an engine is, either.

Toby points to the book and says, "Go on."

"My mom's coming soon," Maureen says. "What time is it?"

Toby can't tell time, but he says, scratching his wrist, "Noon."

"It's not noon," Maureen says. "We already had lunch."

Before my mother married my father, my mother would drive home for lunch, to make sure Maureen was safe. That was when a colored lady used to sing Maureen and Connor songs and cook milk on the stove. Once, the colored lady dropped the bottle of milk, which shattered, and Maureen's mother fired her. Then her mother got married and stayed home all day and never cooked milk, and Maureen started school, and now they lived in Illinois. The State Bird is the cardinal, which is red. Sometimes the cardinal is also Catholic.

She looks at the book and reads, "Jane runs."

"Where?" says Toby. "Turn the page."

Now Mrs. Cameron steps inside the living room. She is wearing a skirt for cooking, wiping her hands on the apron, and says, "*Please*, Toby. *Please* turn the page."

Toby says, "She's holding the book!"

Maureen closes the book and stands up. She pulls up her dark green socks and says, "My mom's coming soon. In her Volkswagen."

−|4−

My father takes his work from the office home, but his extramarital affairs he drops off along the way. Nearby his office stands a hotel, crumbling, though not run-down enough to justify demolition. The lights flicker inside and hum. On the fourth floor, the lovers are high enough above ground to leave open wide the drapes. This way, neither one of them has to touch the fabric.

Mostly, he is flattered. He has always been shy around girls. Working in his garage, drinking his beer, he found it was easier to get things done. To build a chair, or a wooden table. Easier than talking to a female with a brain and involved less risk. With Eve, a girl still in her mid-twenties, who sometimes doesn't wear a bra, because she doesn't need to, with Eve my father feels as if he is somehow entitled to something nice he might deserve. Only afterward, spent, reaching for a cigarette, does he begin to feel naked and foolish. He is, after all, a father and a husband. He is married to a woman who wants to have a garden she will never tend to. He is married to a woman who didn't wait for him to have two kids of her own.

My father says, sitting up on his elbow, "Eve."

"Yes?"

"We forgot to pull the drapes."

"I'm not ashamed," Eve says. "Let the whole world watch."

"No," says my father, reaching for his watch. "You're naked. Eve, it's not time for that." He says, gripping her shoulder, looking her in the eye, "It will never be time for that."

She rests her hand along his thigh, gently, and says, "Well.

Then how about another raise? Quick, before the sun comes up?"

−13−

The cold comfort of fact: a Soviet intermediate-range ballistic missile, or IRBM, has a range of 2,020 nautical miles; once fired from its base in San Cristobal, Cuba, only Seattle is safe. If the US attacks Cuba, an allegedly surgical strike designed strictly to eliminate the missile base, and a couple million citizens, then the Soviets will most likely respond by firing on those Jupiter missile bases in Turkey. To which the US will most likely respond by firing on a Soviet missile base closer to home—Leningrad, or possibly even Moscow. Acheson argues that by then the cooler heads will have had time to sit back and think things out. It's like playing chess badly, this rush into violence. Meanwhile Acheson is on a flight to Paris to keep de Gaulle from feeling left out, and Bobby is having drinks with the Soviet foreign minister Anatoly Dobrynin.

At school, my sister feels left out. At school my sister practices Duck and Cover drills. They sing a song at school, because it's fun to do, like hiding beneath the desk:

> *Duck & Cover, it's the only way*
> *Duck & Cover, to have a sunny day …*

−12−

My father has never been to Paris. The seal will have to be flexible and capable of withstanding several hundred pounds of pressure per square inch. It will also have to be remarkably small. If they can find the correct compounds, possibly it will not leak. My father keeps the sketch with him inside his brief-case on a pad of legal paper.

Each month my father deposits 35 percent of his check into a savings account—close to two hundred dollars. He wants to purchase stock options with the new company in the fall. He wants to save for a down payment on a bigger house. He wants to buy Connor another pair of shoes that Connor will soon grow out of. My mother's Volkswagen also needs a new clutch, which my father will put in by himself next weekend. If he had more money, my father reasons, he wouldn't have to worry about not having any.

My father no longer has any debts, except for those he's re-cently assumed from his new wife. Three hundred dollars for a Volkswagen, which he plans to ditch as soon as he can con-vince his wife they need to. He believes the car is structurally unsafe, as well as expensive. He also needs to finish paying off Connor's maternity bills, which his wife defaulted on two years ago. The cost to change the kids' names was an addi-tional forty-five dollars, each, and Connor needs new shoes. Maureen wants a bike.

His mother, who lives in Florida, writes him often, explain-ing that his own father would be proud. My father is used to taking care of women; it's a job he has experience at. When his own father died, shortly after he was born, his mother moved to Florida and opened up a small hotel. The hotel was worn down, and my father learned to do the maintenance: plumb-ing, hanging sheet rock, running electrical conduit and laying floors. He also learned to avoid running up bills he could not afford.

Eventually, all comes due. My father has, among other things, a genetic flaw locked into the central aorta of his brain. Before his life is over, he will have three cerebral aneurysms, the first of which will strike shortly before his forty-fifth birthday and cause him to spend the next three years of his life relearning how to speak and walk. The surgery to rescue his brain will destroy the faculties of his mind. Years from now, in 1999, after his wife abandons him penniless to the mercy of the state, my father will recall murkily the depths of his wife's black, raven-heart. Then he will fall to the floor in an elevator going up and die.

$-||-$

My father, who art in heaven, distrusts while he is alive the body politic.

He distrusts the body politic more than he does either Kennedy or Nixon. And he understands, my father, that Kennedy won the election on account of those thousands of ballots cast by the Chicago dead—those men and women, still in their graves, resurrected and summoned forth by Daley's Democratic machine. My father, smitten by the inner workings of machines, has to give him credit.

The language of debt is also one of accountability. My mother is uncertain what's on Father Tim's mind, though she suspects it may be lust. While my mother is not particularly influenced by lust—she has, for example, always been in possession of her own orgasm—she does know how to use lust to her advantage. For my mother, sex means needing to wash up afterward: it is typically the kind of sin that can be washed away with prayer so long as nothing is conceived and, consequently, aborted. She also knows that my father is no longer interested. When he comes to bed, he no longer brushes his teeth. His hair is full of axle grease and cigarette smoke and, most recently, a foreign perfume.

Now Father Tim takes my mother's hand across the table. He is not wearing his collar today, and so he appears to be a normal man, capable of sin and respectable amounts of grief. He takes my mother's hand and says, "Linda."

"I love him," my mother says, meaning my father.

"Of course you do," says Father Tim. "Of course you do."

"We're going to move soon," my mother says, beginning to cry. She cries gently at first, gaining momentum. "Do you know why he is doing this?"

"He is a man," says Father Tim, sadly. "The world is going to end?"

"Yes," says my mother, looking at her watch, collecting her wits. "And I am a fucking bitch."

$$-10-$$

My mother couldn't afford a nice briefcase. She had clothes to buy and mouths to feed and she had to pay somebody to look after Connor and Maureen while she went off to work. It's not that my mother doesn't like colored people. When my father asked my mother to marry him, she was making three thousand dollars a year more than he was, and still it was not enough. To pay for the briefcase, she hocked her previous engagement ring, which she had hidden in a shoe to prevent Goose from doing the very same thing. She also skimped on lunch at work.

In Detroit, working for Jackson McDougal Bergson, she wrote an ad for the Pontiac Tempest, which was driven by a trans-axle, something it took my father to explain the meaning of. She decided to focus on the upholstery, and room for kids, and came up with a campaign that even men could admire. For Christmas, her boss gave her a hundred-dollar bonus, based on the success of her ad, and she finally had enough to buy my father's briefcase.

It wasn't leather, but it looked like leather; the snaps were brass and the briefcase had a combination lock. One night, shortly before she moved back to South Bend, she gave it to my father in a box. They were sitting on the floor of my father's apartment because he didn't like to pay for furniture. They lit a fire in the fireplace and my mother went out to her Volkswagen and brought inside a great big box.

"What's this?" my father said, tugging at the ribbons.

"It's a wedding present. For you, Mac."

"Who's it from?"

"Me," my mother said, kissing him. "It's from me."

My father wasn't used to presents. He bought sweaters for his girlfriends, usually *Large*, for Christmas, and for a moment he felt foolish and undeserving. My father was the kind of man who felt more blessed to give, if only because he had never expected to receive, and because of course my father was deeply afraid of debt—spiritual, or otherwise. He knew my mother wanted him to join her church, if only for the kids' sake.

He opened the box, took out the briefcase. "We can't afford this, Linda."

My mother laughed. She said, "We can't afford anything. At least right now. The man said it was the kind of thing you grow into. Like a good sofa. You get used to it."

"Thank you," said my father, frowning.

"It's for your new job. You can't use it until the very first day. Promise."

My father laughed, because there was no possibility for escape. He kissed my mother and said, "Promise. I promise."

"And we need to find a house. With a yard. And a garden!" She said, removing the case from my father's lap, "I've been saving up for that for months."

They threw the ribbons in the fire. They made love that night, my father and my mother. They closed their eyes and fell into a world of promises. They fell into the past, when love was still a state of grace, and not complicity. They fell into each other's arms in order to make love, and a new home, and possibly a family that would last for generations.

—9—

Connor wakes from his nap, startled. He hears wailing in the background—a puppy bumped into by a car: a cat, at night, screaming. The room is dark and his eyes are full of sleep. His head doesn't hurt at all.

In the hallway he searches for the light switch: the light

flashes, for an instant, and burns out. In the dark, blinded only momentarily, he turns into the kitchen, where he finds a tall green bottle and two empty tea mugs and a sugar bowl. Because the country is building highways, his father, who really isn't his father, won't be home for another hour. Then they will have dinner in the big room.

The television only gets one channel, and he is not allowed to watch it. In Ohio, they had three channels, but until they get an antenna, they have just one. He doesn't know yet what precisely an antenna is. When he sits down in front of the television, he is hoping the noises coming from the bedroom will soon stop. He doesn't remember his real father, but he has been taught not to pay attention to the bedroom. Now he stands up, tugs on his pajama bottoms, and enters the dark hallway. When he gets to his mother's bedroom, just outside the door, he sits on the floor and begins to hum.

−8−

She knows how to make a man feel good, particularly a man of God.

−7−

My father is a sad man, though he does not know it. When he becomes sad, he often drinks, and when he cannot drink, he becomes very angry. Anger, his life has taught him, is far more easily controlled. Two years before he dies, he will fall and break his hip. He will have been inside his garage looking for a wrench. After falling inside his empty garage, he will spend the next three hours calling out for help. It is after his wife returns from her weekend trip that she will decide to abandon him entirely, and when my father falls inside his garage, he will be capable of as much thought—sadness, and anger at himself—as possible, given the surgically imposed limitations of his brain. Mercifully, this is long into the future, and because my father cannot see into the future, there is nothing he can do to change it.

Meanwhile, when my father becomes sad, he often thinks of Minnesota, where he was for a brief time happy. In Minnesota, working for Firestone, he lived in a cabin beside a lake. He lived with a crew that did cold-weather testing on the frozen lake— a solid bridge of ice. At night, the men drank fine Canadian whiskey; they played blackjack and whist while telling stories about the day. For hours each day the crew would drive cars across the frozen lake, locking up the brakes, practicing controlled skids. My father would sit behind the wheel of his cold car and drive into the skids, spinning into circles, one after another. His personal record was eleven—too much speed, and one threatened to roll the car proper, even on the ice, and send it crashing through the surface. But driving, driving across the ice, my father knew always he could save himself, there, right before that moment when he accelerated and then thrust himself into oblivion.

−6−

My sister's favorite game is Duck Duck Goose. At school, she and her classmates will sit in a circle, each longing to be singled out. When someone finally taps her on the shoulder, she likes the way that feels. Somebody, anybody, touching her on the shoulder.

She runs like a girl, of course. Outside on the front lawn of Toby Cameron's house, they play freeze tag with Toby's older brother, Doug. Doug is thirteen, and almost too old for tag, and he can outrun them all. Even though it's cold, Doug wears only a sweatshirt, and his face and neck are bright red.

Right now, my sister is frozen still, waiting to be released. Up above, the sky is falling, and a flock of birds is flying south toward Mississippi. She remembers that her father's name is Goose, which is a bird. She remembers that her father never liked to touch her. When he came home, whenever he did come home, he would sit in the kitchen in his underwear. Sometimes he slept loudly on the kitchen floor. Once he made her mommy sick.

Maureen knows that when you are sick, you are not supposed to touch somebody, or share your glass. She shivers, because it's very cold, and because her green socks go up only to her knees. She has a new daddy now, as well as a new name. Waiting on the lawn, frozen, waiting to be released, she tells herself she no longer is a bird.

"I have a new name," she tells herself, stiffly.

It's cold, and the birds in the sky are gone.

"Touch me," she calls to Toby Cameron. "Touch me!"

−5−

My mother says, sitting up, "What time is it?"

Father Tim, naked, looks for his watch. Although he has

slept with my mother often, years ago and typically in Kansas, he has never before lain in my father's bed. He is not used to all the furniture. Over my mother's dressing table, which my father built for her last summer, is a picture of my mother's favorite president. Before she left the Catholic Church, my mother never dreamed she'd be divorced.

And now she's remarried to a man who builds her furniture and sleeps with his secretary on the sly. She sits up naked, looking at Tim, who after the fact appears childish and small. Her mouth tastes like wine and smoke and sweat.

"Oh my God," Tim whispers. "Here we go again."

My mother says, lifting the sheets, swinging naked off the bed, "No. You have to dress. Before I hurt you even more."

On the way to the hallway, she stops at her dressing table, and reaches for her brush.

$$-4-$$

Time flies. My father, the man who taught me to speak, and to think, the man who taught me to see—my father is naturally worried about the future, given that it is his responsibility to protect his family from it. Eyeball to eyeball, says the secretary of state. When my father drops Eve off at her El station, he doesn't wave good-bye.

Neither Khrushchev nor Kennedy wants a war. Neither wants to admit mistakes, either. Theirs is a marriage of diplomatic immunity. The Jupiter missiles in Turkey are obsolete; they should have been removed long before when Kennedy in fact ordered them to be removed. Meanwhile, Russian warships have been sent to Cuba, and even the brothers Kennedy believe the blockade is going to escalate: war, it appears, is inevitable, and my father is stuck in traffic. While he has never met a citizen of the Soviet Union, my father feels no particular hostility toward that union. Never before has the world felt so cold.

How to undo this knot of war? My father is on the executive fast track. First he is going to build for the world an air adjustable shock absorber, and then he will do the obligatory MBA at the University of Chicago, and he will ascend the ranks, smartly, and pile away those options. But right now, and long before he becomes the corporate second-in-command, his is a fragile career that shall rely on his ability to engineer a soft ride and unprecedented comfort. In the meantime, the heater on his '53 Ford—a hole, really, blowing in hot air from the engine—is failing to warm the car. Because the traffic has not moved a hundred feet in the past fifteen minutes, the interior has become cold to the touch. Speed helps to keep things warm, even when one is uncertain of his or her direction: if my father leaves my mother, he will not settle down with Eve, and in just that moment, that moment when he is reaching into his breast pocket for a cigarette and match, he makes his decision: it's the kind of choice he's been raised by experience to make. Meanwhile, the match flickers, brightly, and he breathes in the sulfur and examines the flame he's holding by his fingertips, which warms them, briskly.

Up ahead, a Caterpillar tractor is clearing away the road, and finally the cars begin to move. My father shifts into second, which provides him with sufficient torque to proceed, when suddenly the traffic stops again. A green car behind him hits his bumper, and my father smashes his hand into the steering wheel. The cigarette has burned his fingers.

He has to turn around to see, because there is no rearview mirror, and when he does so he sees a tall man in boots and jeans and a heavy coat striding up to his window. The window doesn't work, it will not cooperate, and so my father opens the door, and the man slams it shut. The man is yelling at my father for driving like an old lady.

My father's mother, who is an old lady, no longer drives, though he thinks she still may have a car somewhere in Florida. My father attempts to open the door again, his fingers hot, smarting, and again the man slams the door, and when this happens, when the door slams and bangs my father's knee, and when he considers the current state of traffic—gridlocked— he allows himself to become angry. It is not a difficult decision, and he is glad for so justifiable an occasion. The blood is rushing to his head now, where a vein begins to throb, pumping the adrenaline, and now when he pushes against the door, he does so quickly, and takes the man by surprise.

The door hits the man in the knees, and he steps back. The man begins to say something and my father feels the ice in the wind, slapping his face, cutting through his overcoat. Standing outside on a dirt road full of holes, beside his old car, he thinks he must resemble a bank teller, or possibly an unemployed pharmacist: his coat is dark, and lightweight, and very thin.

The man says something, loudly, and people are beginning to pay attention. Men mostly, eager for a fight, bored with all the traffic, though secretly hoping that if a fight breaks out, each will not be expected to become involved except for the man in jeans and boots, glaring. When my father coldcocks him, the man falls to his knees. My father's hand hurts, naked in the raw cold, and he decides not to wait for the man to rise. Instead, my father hits him again, somewhere on a tooth, because now his knuckles begin to bleed. The man is covering his face, whimpering, and my father lifts him by the shoulder and slams the man's face into the trunk of my father's secondhand '53 Ford. The man falls to the dirt and nobody seems to be paying any mind, though of course everybody is. Everybody is watching from behind their windshields, careful of being caught watching. Now my father lifts the man and drags him back to his green car. He opens up the door. He helps the man inside and shuts the door.

My father returns to his car, shaking, though he no longer feels the cold. Instead he reaches for his cigarettes. Mostly, he feels naked and foolish, the way he does after ejaculating into Eve's mouth. Right now he is grateful for the high collar on his coat, which causes him to feel as if he is a spy. He rolls up the collar and pulls the Ford onto a snow-covered lawn. He cuts a corner, then another, until he finally finds a bar while shifting into third.

-3-

Connor is cold, sitting in the hallway. He has wandered to the other end, far away from the door, and he can't remember any songs he knows the words to. Sitting in the hallway, his feet tucked under his thighs, he waits for the bedroom door to open. While he waits in the dark, he plays I Spy by himself.

I spy a silver pony, he tells himself. *Where?*

When the door opens, my mother steps into the hall and flicks on the light, which is burned out. She turns and reaches for the bathroom light. She is naked, holding her brush, her skin musty and warm, utterly alive. When she sees Connor, sitting in the hallway, she drops the brush onto the floor. The floors are cold, made of hard wood, and she stands there looking at her son.

"I couldn't sleep," Connor says. "I was tired."

He begins to cry, frightened, and now my mother kneels before him. She takes him in her arms and says, "Mommy was taking a nap."

"I know. But Mommy wasn't tired."

She lifts him up, into her arms, and carries him into his bedroom. She sits him on his bed and says, "Mommy has to change."

"Okay."

She says, "We *both* have to change, or Daddy won't like us." She says, tugging off his pajama bottoms, "Let's race."

In the bathroom, alone, she brushes her hair and teeth. She steps inside the bedroom and tells Father Tim to get out of the way. While she dresses, she tells Father Tim to sit still in the wooden chair beside the dressing table. Now she pulls back the bedspread and removes the sheets. She throws the sheets onto the floor and locates a new set and makes the bed all over again. Having performed his service, Father Tim has now become a burden and a tax. When he rises to help with the sheets, she says, "No. Sit down," and she gives him orders to leave when she has left the rented house. Do not touch a thing, she says. You are to go out the door and far away from here.

"Linda," says Father Tim. "Linda …"

"No," my mother whispers. "Like a ghost, Tim. Like your precious, holy ghost."

−2−

Spirits haunt, thank God—

I will be named after the president of these United States— JFK. Jack, my father will call me. Little Jack.

And later, after I have grown, Jack.

Father Tim, the man who stumbled into my conception, his collar briefly removed, will never speak my name.

My mother, a raven-hearted woman, has coal black hair down to her waist. Though she cannot conjugate a verb to save her life, she has two years toward a degree in French literature at a teachers' college, and she has also been repeatedly beaten by a man she married in order to be rich but who instead gave her syphilis. My mother has two kids of her own, Connor and Maureen, who have by now become my brother and my sister. She tells herself that she loves a man who builds her furniture and that a son of his own will keep him home. When she first met my father in Pittsburgh, years ago, his slacks were torn at the knee.

My father went to what was then called Carnegie Tech. He wanted to be an engineer, and he wanted to go to college, and he paid his way by cutting lumber in the Northeast. He tended bar for his fraternity. He worked as a mechanic in a shop just across the Allegheny River. When he graduated, his mother presented him with a bill for $13,700.

Everything was itemized. So many dollars for ice cream. So many dollars for basketballs and baseballs and tools, like wrenches and hammers. A list for school clothes. Another for food. His mother said there wasn't any particular rush to pay her back.

It took ten years, often working nights. By the time he was thirty-two, he had paid his mother off with interest—4.5 percent—and when he married, he insisted on a courtroom wedding. No church, no songs, no reason to invite anybody he didn't care to. Particularly his mother.

Instead his mother read about it in a small clipping from a newspaper in South Bend. My mother, before she sent it off, enclosed a short note:

Now he's mine. No need to send a gift.

−|−

The history of conflict is the history of the pointed finger, and to point your finger is to allow for the possibility of contact. Just who do we really have to blame? The genetic flaw within the fabric of my father's brain is presently invisible to medical science. While Acheson is off in Paris, briefing de Gaulle to keep either from feeling left out, Bobby Kennedy is having drinks with Anatoly Dobrynin. Bobby promises to have the Jupiter missiles removed from Turkey so long as Moscow promises not to leak the deal.

My mother wants to keep her husband. My father wants

to have a son. Nations have been built on lesser inclinations. The hill leading up to Toby Cameron's house is fairly steep, and my mother's Volkswagen is lugging near the top. Once in the driveway, an hour late to pick her daughter up, my mother rolls down the window and toots the horn.

"Maureen," she calls, across the lawn. "Maureen!"

Connor sits in the backseat, silent. His mother has promised ice cream, and he wants her to keep her promise. Maureen runs across the lawn, stopping only once to tug her green socks up. Once inside the car, the two of them tucked into the back, my mother insists on making her apology. She insists on practicing. She insists on stopping at the store for a nice bottle of Canadian whiskey and next she's going to order pizza for the kids and she's going to go to bed early with a headache.

"I'm sorry," my mother says, for the seventh time. "I lost track of time."

Maureen says, "We read the same book. Twice!"

Connor, who cannot read a whit, bangs his head against the window. He gazes blankly out the window at the sky.

My mother, turning up the heat, reminds herself that first she needs to bathe. She says, setting her lip, "No. Oh God, please. Please forgive me."

My mother, having borne thus far two children, no longer associates shame with any particular act of the body. Instead she blames the will, the secret intent to deceive, and possibly destroy. And it is not shame, or the scent of her lover in her hair, that leads her to this conviction.

It is love, and the fact that I have now been conceived by more than just a fine idea. The Big Bang. When my father's brain explodes, in 1976, it will feel just like that. It is a love, my mother's, limited by the prescriptions of her black and narcissistic heart. *God the father, God the son*, my mother thinks. *Who's to ever know?* It's an idea she will have to spend her life keeping secret. It's an idea she's going to hold inside the palm of her hand until it simply melts away.

Tonight around the moon there is a ring.

$$-0-$$

Why does a man tell another's story? To locate his own.

Perhaps it is Time that loses track of us. Between the here and now, perhaps Time is merely content to suspend the living. The Monroe Doctrine, declared in 1823, states specifically that no other nations will be permitted to extend their influence on the Western Hemisphere; it also promises to keep the US out of Europe. At the time it was a toothless document, like an insurance policy, but things change, and people like my father invent telephones and automobiles and airplanes, and the Era of Good Feelings passes into the modern world of the Marshall Plan and Checkpoint Charlie. My father, meanwhile, works for a company that manufactures machine guns and washing machines and automotive mufflers. Incidentally, Maryvale's chief competitor in the automotive industry is a company that also bears that same name.

Monroe. When you want to feel secure, you drive Monroe.

How to explain such confluence? Such moments of convergence? My father believes in competition, because competition creates a better product; he has a job only because he is in fact expected to design the world's first air adjustable shock absorber that will rely on the seal he makes to withstand the weight of the family car. It's a matter of national security, knowing where your interests lie. In Chicago, they say *cahrr,* and while my father is uncertain of those historical currents that have brought his family to the brink of thermonuclear war, he does know that he is sitting in a bar, his hands trembling, and ordering another boilermaker. *Fast track,* the people at work say about him, pointing. Truth is, all he ever really wanted to do was race—motorcycles, stock cars—and on the television above the bar, which appears to receive more channels than his own at home, he watches a newscaster read from a freshly typed piece of paper. The world, says the anchorman, holds its breath.

Who shall be the first to blink? To look the other way? Who shall be the first to cast the stone? My father tells himself that now is not a time to be getting stoned. When my father lights a cigarette, smoke rises into his eyes.

He wipes the blood from his knuckles onto his coat. His hands, he has come to realize, smell like another woman. He will have to wash his hands, he thinks. He will have to keep them in his pockets and to himself. When he went flying out of a second-story window, in college, he cut his face up in the glass. Sitting at the bar, looking into the mirror, he sees his face, and the scar running down along his face, and he remembers the way my mother, Linda, dressed his wounds. Days later he asked her to cut the stitches out, by herself, in order to save eight dollars. One night, after he could walk, they went to a joint for pizza and beer. They ordered a pitcher of beer, and when it arrived, my mother asked my father if he was going to pour her a glass.

"Best to pour your own," my father said. "Especially if you plan to drink it."

At first she thought he meant it as an insult; he could see it in her eyes. She poured herself a glass, and they sat there, talking, and he began to pay attention to her eyes. They were pretty eyes, dark and uncomplicated, merely manipulative in their transparent way. Looking into her eyes, he didn't feel shy. Even if his face was cut up, even if he had gone flying through a window, even if he didn't have a home, here was someone he could make one with. Two orphans, drinking from a pitcher of beer in Pittsburgh, Pennsylvania: it was the kind of opportunity he told himself he'd need to look for, later on, after he'd paid his dues.

Now his hands carried the scent of another woman, and he is sitting in a bar, and his knuckles are bloody and torn. It is late, and he knows his wife will be worried about the traffic. When he stands, he pours down his beer, and because the joint also sells package goods, my father asks for a quart of Meister Brau to go. He is calm now, after feeling foolish, still shaken, and he imagines for an instant that kind of world that will no longer bear his name. He is an only child, the last of his line. He reaches for his briefcase, on the stool beside him, which holds his detailed sketch.

"End of the line," he says to the bartender, wiping his eyes.

"End of the fucking world," says the bartender. "Better dead than red."

And my father says, tucking the bottle of beer up under his arm, "Not hardly."

Because secretly he believes he is capable of making this world a safer place, and this specifically is what he longs for. A chance, just one, to do more. In the car, he breaks open the beer, takes a pull, and starts his engine. It's going to be a gamble, he thinks, either way. In the distance, there is a long, heavy cable being raised into the winter sky by men working overtime. Like the Indiana Skyway, it has always been possible to connect one state with another, and what my father is telling himself now is that tomorrow he will have to be a better man. Tomorrow he will have to strike a bargain; he will have to ask Eve to find another boss, perhaps someone in sales. Then he will ask Linda if he can sell the Volkswagen. He will offer to take the train, so she can have the car, and he will promise to be home on time for at least the entire week.

To make an engine work, you have to give it fuel. You have to give it air. You have to give it space to breathe. My father is good with tools, and he is good with his hands. It's something Linda tells him often ... *You're good with your hands, Mac* ... and my father knows that tonight is shot. Not tonight, but maybe tomorrow night, or the next, long after dark. After the kids are all asleep, maybe then he will turn to her in the night, the way he used to. He will turn to her—his hand on her hip, bridging the distance—and whisper to her without apology. Then, after a while, he will settle near her ribs, waiting for a spark, because this is what he understands. To fill a woman with desire, it's important you respect the body; you have to give it reason to provide you with a home. You have to give her hope that you will at least try to be a decent man. My father, who is thirty-three during the fourth week of October 1962, my father wants to raise a family in America. He wants to play a little baseball with his firstborn son. He wants to teach me how to drive. He wants to raise a family in America because he knows that time is running out.

Tonight there is a ring around the moon.

OPEN MY HEART

T he boy in the burn unit had been weeping silently, which is why nobody on the nightshift had noticed. His pillow was damp and smelled like seawater. She had seen before the tears running from the corners of his eyes. Mornings, while she bathed the boy, he tried to be cheerful. It was important, she understood, always to be gentle. He had the body of a seventeen-year-old—capable, certainly, but not yet the solid mass of a grown man. She drew the cool, cotton cloth across the nipples on his chest, the tender rib cage, and on toward his navel. From there a thin ribbon of blond hair, occasionally blotted out by fresh scar tissue, led to his loins—a road to heaven. But once there his genitals and pubic region were simply scarred beyond all recognition. Red, angry, the scar tissue raising itself insistently as it healed. *Proud flesh.* The boy had been here now for several months. She adjusted his catheter, which was constantly slipping from the knob of flesh which constituted the remains of his penis.

As she made the adjustment, the surgical plastic digging into his urethra, the boy cried out.

"There," she said, patting his elbow, one of the few places on his body not seared by the fire. "There."

"Thank you," said the boy. "I'm sorry."

"Nonsense," she said. "We are going to make you better. How many glasses of water?"

"Two," said the boy.

"I'll bring you another. Your sister is here. She brought flowers. Dr. Nick says you're well enough for flowers. They're lovely."

"Susie?"

"Yes?"

"I won't get an infection? I mean, any more?"

"No," she said. "You're healing fine," and she drew the sheet up to his waist. She waved aside a lock of her own hair and leaned down to kiss him on the forehead. "Don't be sad," she said, kissing him, and then she left the room.

Later that morning she had a conversation with the plastic surgeon who would be reconstructing the boy's penis. The testicles had been consumed by the fire, gone to smoke and ash, but the doctor seemed hopeful he might be able to lend a degree of normalcy to the boy through a series of reconstructive surgeries. These were miraculous times. In Louisville an amputee had just recently been given a new hand with which to touch his wife. Fingers had become easy to reattach so long as one located them quickly. Despite the thinness of the boy, his relatively small size, there appeared to be a viable amount of material to harvest from his buttocks and thighs.

"How is he," said the doctor.

"His spirits are low," she said. "But his sister came to visit. I thought I'd try another book."

"The Jesus freak?"

"Yes," she said. She watched the doctor struggle to keep his eyes from gazing at her breasts. It was a routine they passed each time they spoke. He was handsome and prosperous and good at what he did—a beautiful wife, two happy children; he was also at risk of falling in love with her. Were she a cruel woman, she would have permitted him to trip.

His eyes met her own, and he averted his eyes to her ears, then her hair, and then the fire extinguisher located in the wall behind her. To meet a woman's gaze was dangerous for a man—it left him naked, unprepared for the suddenness of possible invitation. Now his eyes fell again toward her cleavage, then rose immediately, embarrassed by the possibility of having been caught looking. It was the sign of a good man, she knew. He would look, because he simply could not help himself, but he would never linger, and he would always, always apologize afterward by stepping back, turning his head, this way, then that—anywhere but here, the center of her chest.

A plastic surgeon, a man who biweekly performed two dozen silicon implants, even he could not be made not to look. Like it or not, her husband would say, it was a law of geometry. A man leads with his chin; a woman, the tip of her breast. A good man, she knew, would steal a glance at a woman and save it up for later.

When you were left alone, only then would it be safe to look at what you'd seen—a passerby who'd caught your eye, or a particular vision of another's life. Granted, too, she knew she could have dressed more quietly, but she did not like to wear a lot of clothes, especially in the heat of Phoenix, and she *did* like to feel the sun on her chest. She liked fine cotton and silk sundresses. She liked the fact of her skin, and the air and water which moved against it. At work, she conceded to the uniform and wore her lab coat; but once into the world, she liked to feel as undressed to the elements as the world might actually permit. Her husband, who understood the elements of fashion far better than she, would underscore at times like this the fundamental premise of all fabric—that which conceals, also reveals. There was no fabric known to man more essential than the skin upon his body.

Or hers, she would say, reminding him. Her husband, who was a good man, a man who generally preferred Cerruti to Zegna, said she wore her heart upon her sleeve. At home, she walked through the house, briefly checking the mail on the dry sink; she stepped out to the backyard, where she removed her sandals and then her dress, which she hung upon a lamp. The sky was brilliantly white, the desert sun at its peak. The heat around her wrapped her up. She slid off her underwear and slipped her body into the pool, the water defining the very heat around her, and then she slid her head beneath the water. She returned to take a breath. A deep breath, and she thought about her husband, seventeen years her senior, who would be in Rome now. She fell in love with him when she was just a girl. Seventeen, the age of the boy on her ward. The boy had a road to heaven, same as she. Eight years ago, she began electrolysis treatments, thinking to please her husband. Then he surprised her, the first time in several months, and asked her to desist. He loved the stripe of fur, he explained, as well as the few vagrant strands of hair upon her nipples—and he made her promise never, never to have reconstructive surgery, which was then becoming popular even in the West outside of California. He said, placing his hand upon her breast, "Let them drift, let them curve. Let them be."

Of course she hadn't had any children, and she'd been twenty-four at the time, a set of particular circumstances which would make it far easier for a man to insist on his beloved following nature's course. This, too, during a time when they made love regularly. She still didn't have any children, and this lack was beginning to annoy her. While she wasn't certain, she believed he was increasingly made nervous by, among other things, his lack of stamina. Not that he wasn't in fine shape, but fine shape at fifty wasn't thirty-four. She was seventeen when she fell in love with him, seventeen years ago, when he was thirty-four—they'd been together the same amount of time the world had taken to make the boy with the mutilated genitalia. She'd married her husband in Cambridge after she'd finished college. He brought flowers—a lei, orchids and plumerias, shipped overnight from Oahu—to her graduation and draped them around her neck.

To remind themselves of the possibility of the ocean, they had insisted on the pool being treated with a salt chlorination system, which in turn caused the water to feel like silk. Saltwater, they reasoned, was good for the skin—cuts healed more swiftly—which is why the body shed saltwater to begin with—through the pores, through the very eyes. The garden needed watering, she thought. And she loved the heat, the sun on the back of her neck, and knees. She lifted herself from the pool, the water dripping from her body. She would need to water the bougainvillea and the oleanders in the garden. She loved the fact of water, and she missed her husband, who most likely had a new lover in Italy.

She wanted him to hurry home. She wanted him to hurry home to her and take her in the pool.

What makes marriage possible? A willingness to be perfectly honest—tastes, habits, fantasies, mistakes. Also a willingness not to punish your partner for those very same tastes, habits, fantasies, mistakes that you insist on knowing. She loved her husband to the quick: that he should have a mistress in a foreign country caused her distress, to be certain, but she would never punish him unnecessarily for it, if only because to do so would destroy the very fabric of the marriage, and that was sacred. The marriage—the union of each—was inviolable, built upon, to use her husband's language, a commitment guided by reason and law. The heart was a sacred object, necessary to protect—by the ribs, by the fabric of our public lives—if only because the heart insisted on following the paradoxical rules of its own making. The heart's desire was not necessarily the mind's. Her husband, who in the initial stages of their courtship would often masturbate beside her, sometimes coming between her breasts, or against the small of her back ... at first she had been surprised. But she had also been seventeen, and then everything had been brand-new. Eventually, she had begun instructing his hand, just so, here and there, often in the spirit of efficiency. A quick fifteen-minute trip, just before rising to leave for work. A car ride home from a tedious business dinner. They had learned she understood to work together.

They had learned to work together because a deep marriage is an efficient one guided by trust, and lust, and mercy. Because a deep marriage is one that understood its depths.

Made in heaven, you hoped. It was the woman in Italy who threw things off balance, and before that, the one in Paris. He explained. He explained that these women required nothing from him—except for gifts, and sometimes cash. He explained he might be tired, and lonely, and he explained he was too old a rooster to change his ways. He explained they helped him to sleep.

"But why won't you make love to me?"

"Because with you I have to please, and sometimes I just can't. I just can't, Susie. A wannabe model in Paris," he said, "I don't make love to that. It is not the same. She fucks me, thinking I'll introduce her to Lagerfeld, and I fuck her, thinking I'll never, never do this again." He said, "Either way, it is not about you."

"It is if it hurts me," she said. "I see it, you know. Sometimes. I can actually *see* you in bed with another woman. The way she bites your lip? You can't imagine."

"Then stop looking," he said. "Because that will make you angry, and anger will destroy us."

"Poison," she said. "The pus beneath the blister?"

And so she had agreed not to raise a fuss, so long as the terms were clear. First, she must always know. Second, nobody else must ever know. Third, he must promise to leave her—Susie—the moment he understood he wanted to.

She, too, would do likewise. She'd had a brief affair with a surgeon from the third floor—a cardiologist, named Bigg, but he was looking for a wife. Too, he was insufferably correct. He was a short, fit man, with the name of Bigg, a name he wore upon his breast as if it were equivalent to Guggenheim or Givenchy. He was, after all, recognized across the world for his surgical skill. Among other things, he thought she should be a doctor. He wanted to send her to medical school.

"No," she said.

They were sitting on the eighth floor of the Hyatt. The air-conditioning was blasting through the ductwork. They were sitting naked on the bed picking at a plate of fruit. It was afternoon, and he would have to return soon to the hospital for his rounds.

"You could go anywhere," he said. "With your experience."

"No," she said. "I like to make people feel better; that's my job. To comfort. Sometimes, I hold a woman's hand, or arm—she's been blown up in a car wreck, or set her house on fire, drunk, smoking in bed—doesn't matter. People burn themselves up every day. But if you can find a healthy patch of flesh, and just touch her. Just that—it's a gift, one I'm good at. I make people feel better," she said. "People who will be disfigured beyond their own mothers' recognition—"

"You'd make more money," her doctor said. "More responsibility. People would respect you."

On the way to the hotel, she had stopped at the Shell station, and her hands still smelled like gasoline. She said, looking him in the eye, "Respect is more than a half dozen terrified interns kissing your ass. I've seen doctors. I've seen the way you treat anybody you deign beneath you. Even veterinarians, it's shameful. A doctor steps into the examining room and says,

never extending a hand, I'm Dr. So-and-So, you know you're
dealing with an asshole, pure and simple. As for money," she
said, reaching for a strawberry, "after how much is it okay to
stop worrying about it? What, I'm going to drive a Jaguar? My
husband's rich. My father was rich. A very nice thing about
being rich is not having to buy a Jaguar, if you know what I
mean."

He said, "You should be a doctor. The profession needs
you."

And she said, getting off the bed, "You're not listening, are
you?"

"Your husband might divorce you—"

"Well, he might. Or I might him. It's always a given choice
which makes any decision possible. Enough," she said, stepping into the bathroom, "is enough, don't you think?"

And then she peed. She had left the door open so he could
listen. After rinsing her face, she dressed, and then she left for
the elevator. At the concierge she stopped and left a note ad-
dressed to her Dr. Bigg.

Sorry to be so bitchy, she wrote. *I was lonely.*

A woman who wears Natori lingerie, she knows what she
wants, or so her husband would have the world believe. What
you see is what you get. He was in Rome now consulting the
board of Gucci about positioning itself against Louis Vuitton's
hostile takeover bid. Months ago, he'd seen this coming.

That night, after her run, after her dinner of salad and soup,
she went to their bed. There she called her husband's hotel. He
wasn't in, of course—time changed the way one felt all across

the world. She thought of that line from the poet Robert Hass, *Longing, we say, because desire is full of endless distances.* She said into her husband's voice mail, "I was really hoping you'd be there. I was hoping you could help me out."

She said, "I love you. And I want you to love me back."

In the morning, she woke, and took her morning dip. She chose a navy dress with spaghetti straps, and then a cashmere cardigan to fight the hospital air-conditioning, which always caused the early part of a day to feel as if she were inside a refrigerator. At 10:00, the cooling system would finally kick off.

The boy's sister was waiting for her. She wore a silver bracelet in honor of the unborn. She was reading the Bible, from the looks of her bookmarked place, something from the New Testament, post-Gospels. The girl smiled the drug-induced smile of those persistently enthralled by the Holy Spirit. Her T-shirt said, *Young Life!*

Susie said good morning to the girl.

"He's better," the girl said. "In spirits." The girl said, crossing her arms against the cold refrigeration, "I prayed for him again all last night."

"Yes," Susie said, nodding. "That was very thoughtful."

"It's the sin," the girl said. "He was filled with sin, and shame. Jesus takes our shame away from our bodies. He's better now. No more lusting."

"Excuse me?"

"On account of, you know. His. His—"

"Testicles," Susie said, gently. "It's not a dirty word."

"Yes," said the girl. Susie now understood that the girl was embarrassed by her erect nipples, which were poking through the lettering of her T-shirt. "I told him," the girl said, as if hoping to change the subject, "he can always adopt. Later on, after he gets married. Personally I think he should go to Bible College and become a pastor."

"You do?"

"Jesus saved him," the girl said. "For a *reason*."

Susie sat beside the girl and shivered, crossing her own arms, and then her legs. She said, "You are here on vacation?"

"Uh huh. Then back for my semester internship. I am being called to North Carolina."

"It's beautiful there," Susie said. "The mountains."

The girl began to cry. Her open Bible fell from her lap to the floor, and Susie picked it up for her. She saw that the place was marked, and closed it. The Bible was stuffed with notes and small pieces of paper indicating essential passages. The girl wiped her face on the sleeve of her T-shirt, and then Susie, after setting aside the Bible, put her arm around the girl. She wished she could at least remember the girl's name.

"There," Susie said.

The girl began to recover. "He likes you, and Dr. Sanders. He says everybody is always nice. But he says you're his favorite."

"He is everybody's favorite," Susie said. "So sweet. He gets the very best care. The very best."

"Our dad—he won't visit him. And now Mom lives in Florida. And the insurance is all run out. The plastic surgery … how can he afford that?"

"It's been worked out," Susie said. "The surgeon is volunteering. It's called pro bono. Like I said, everybody likes him—"

"He thought he had lice," the girl said. "Crabs?"

"Yes."

"They made him itch. He thought he'd have to go to the doctor. He was scared of the doctors." She began to cry again. She said, wiping her eyes, "Before. Before I gave my life to Jesus, I used to sin. I mean a lot. But Christ's blood gave me back my virginity. I mean, I am a virgin in Christ's eyes—because He, you know. He took the pain of the cross."

"You believe this in your heart?"

"I do," said the girl, nodding. "I know you're not a Christian. I can tell. But lots of sophisticated people are saved later on. Even Paul. Just like Paul."

"Saint Paul," Susie said, thinking, *Crystal. Her name is Crystal.* She said, "Crystal, I think God will forgive your brother long before your brother forgives himself. I don't think God was ever angry to begin with. I think it's very important your brother not dwell on guilt, and sin. Mostly he needs to feel loved."

"But God's love—"

"And yours," Susie said. "Which is directed by God. Bring him flowers

—freesias, especially. The way they smell."

"He tried to kill himself. That's what people say."

"He tried to cure himself, and he was scared, and lonely, and now he's in the burn unit. This is not about you, Crystal."

"But I told him. I told him it was a sin. I told him, sexual lice is the vermin of Satan!"

"No," Susie said. "You told him how you felt. And he told us how he felt. But nobody, nobody ever makes us speak."

She rose and, after making sure Crystal knew her way to the cafeteria, excused herself. At the nursing station, she learned that the married man in 605 had died last night. His wife was expected later, as well as his three children, because they drove in each weekend from Amarillo. They were still on the road. By now they would be near Flagstaff.

There was also a message for her from David, wanting to have lunch. He was an Anglican priest, with whom she had dallied, off and on, after leaving Dr. Bigg on the eighth floor of the Hyatt. David was easier, if only because he too was married, as well as literate. Often they had read together in bed.

Sharon, the new nurse, asked her when her husband would be back.

After Thanksgiving, she said. Three more weeks. Then Bangkok in December.

The nurse was perplexed, of course. Certainly the nurse would never permit *her* husband to travel abroad like that. And why work, while on the subject, anyway? And why here? Her husband was a school teacher in Tempe. They were going to buy a semicustom house with loads of upgrades and amenities in Ahwatukee. And have kids, properly.

Perhaps if her husband were not sterile, things might be different. Susie could never be certain. She considered sometimes having a baby. David, for example, would make for a fine genetic line, but in general she was uncertain of her need to bring another life into an already overpopulated world. It seemed faintly self-indulgent, insisting that any child she raise must belong to her by blood. Her husband, despite his protestations that he would not be hurt, that he would welcome the new life into his home, regardless of paternity—she knew, too, he *would* be hurt, and she knew he would resent the upheaval in their life: diapers, nannies, diapers—lots of crying late at night. And whenever she arrived this far in her thinking, she knew she wanted to be pregnant, and swollen: sick in the mornings, starving by night. She knew she wanted to feed a baby from her breast. And she knew, likewise, she was running out of time, and that she must be absolutely certain this particular baby was not being invented for the purposes of assuaging her loneliness, or for ratcheting up the territorial boundaries of their marriage. If she was lucky, maybe she could have both, her husband and her child. But if it came down to either, she would pick her husband.

The risk, of course, was that her husband would leave her anyway. And it struck her, just then, that she was afraid this might be happening at this very moment.

Shock is caused by surprise, which is caused by not knowing. It's why the eyes dilate—to see more. She felt her heart palpitate. David, she knew, would be on the floor later, making his rounds—the woman in 611 was from his parish: during a monsoon, last August, a microburst had caused a power line to brush against the lap of her thighs. The neighbors found her skirt hanging from a mesquite tree.

A bolt of lightning, a bolt of cloth … each heightened equally the body's essential nakedness. She went to the boy's room. He was attempting to defecate, and she waited outside, listening to the clenched, tangled violence of his bowels. She entered first the bathroom and ran the tap, and before the boy knew it she had stepped outside of the bathroom and scooped away the bedpan, out of sight.

Later, after washing him, she sat by his bed.

"I had a nice talk with your sister," she said. "She loves you very much."

He nodded shyly. "Dr. Nick saw me last night. He brought me that," he said, pointing to a Diamondbacks cap. "When I get better he said we can go to a game. He's going to do the first operation day after tomorrow."

"He's sweet," she said. "He sure does love the Diamond-backs."

"It's 'cause my dad never visits," he said. "It's okay. I mean, Dr. Nick doesn't have to take me to a game or anything."

She said, "Have you ever heard of Patrick O'Brian?"

"No. Is he an actor?"

"He writes these books about the sea. Lots of battle and gunpowder. My husband loves them."

"My English teacher brings me books, too. I'm all caught up now. I mean, I won't be held back or anything. Next year I am going to graduate on time, even."

"That's wonderful," she said.

"Uh huh. I've read *All Quiet on the Western Front* and *The Red Badge of Courage* and *The Scarlet Letter.*"

"*The Scarlet Letter*?"

"It was a movie, last year. I mean the book came first."

Susie said, carefully, "It was written a long time ago. People sure did think a lot differently then."

"I guess," he said. He said, looking out the window, "I can't have any children. It's cool, I guess. I mean, that could never happen to me now."

Pearl, she thinks. Hester's little girl was named *Pearl*.

The day to day, the lives she intersects with her very own—the stories here will break your heart. Loneliness, she thinks, is what endangers a marriage most. It is the root of all distractions. Of course, it is also what makes possible your ability to join—if not with one, then with another. Mouth to mouth, to the hip, by the balls of your feet. Truth is, she likes to be alone, and then she loves to reunite. She wants to be hungry before she eats a meal. She thinks, I am getting lonely.

She thinks, *He's leaving me.*

On the way out of the hospital with David, they passed Crystal, who was bringing in more flowers.

"I got the freesias," she said. "They *do* smell pretty." Then Crystal turned to David, who was wearing his collar. "Hi," Crystal said to him, beaming.

"Will I see you again?" Susie asked.

"I don't know, ma'am. I have to catch my bus later this afternoon."

"Well then," Susie said, stepping forward. She removed the flowers from Crystal's arms, passed them to David, and embraced her. She hugged the girl to her bones. She kissed her cheek, and said, stepping back, "Look at me."

"Okay," Crystal said, nodding.

"It is not your fault. What happened to your brother. You did not cause it."

Then Susie took the flowers from David and returned them to the girl. "If you hurry, you can get lunch. Macaroni and cheese. Strawberry ice cream."

"Thank you," said the girl, and as she scampered away, Susie understood that someday the girl would know a little bit more. She would have a husband, and a family. Someday she might become a nurse, assuming her bus didn't crash, or she wasn't seduced by her pastor. Assuming there were no surprises, which there would be. Still, looking at the girl, she understood the girl was presently out of danger. It was something she just knew.

At lunch, she ordered a green chili quesadilla, which would cause her agony, later on. She loved green chilis, but she would nonetheless be miserable through the next digestive cycle. She also ordered a vodka martini.

After ordering the very same, David said, "I thought you didn't drink."

"Only when I'm lonely."

The martini tasted flammable, which David explained was on account of the vermouth. He talked for a while about his sons, his wife's endless struggles with the parish wives. He said, after a while, his eyes falling to her chest, "I'm boring you?"

"No," she said, smiling gently. She said, "You know, I spend all day, touching people. I like that. I do. But sometimes I want to be touched back."

He took her hand, reaching across the table.

"No," she said, laughing. "That's not what I mean. And I

don't mean I want to be laid, either. I mean I'm afraid someday nobody will want to. When I'm old. You go to a nursing home—who ever, ever hugs these people? And on the ward—that woman with the thighs. She's lucky, but she won't think so when her husband sees the damage. A power line!"

"He was pretty shook up," David said. "Apparently her heart stopped. He had to punch her half a dozen times in the chest. Kept breaking her ribs. It tore him up."

"Precordial thump," she said. "It's designed to start the heart back up." She said, pushing away her drink, "If you and I went and got a room and got it on, right now, that would be nice. But you still couldn't tell your wife. She'd be hurt, crushed, she'd be betrayed et cetera. And your kids would find out. And all the time we are making love, you are thinking about your wife, and how you'll have to remove the smell of my perfume from your hair. Your collar."

"Well, yeah. But we've been there before."

"And then there's the possibility you bump into my husband. In a parking lot. At the symphony?"

"So," David said. "So?"

"He's going to leave me. I think. He's going to leave me because he feels guilty about his women and because he knows I want a baby."

"He doesn't have to treat you like this, you know. You do not have to accept it."

"Accept what? I love him. I could love you, or another, and I do love you, but not the way I love him. And right now I love *him*. You know, sometimes, before, I used to go to your services. I wanted to hear you give a sermon. And your wife, she's absolutely beautiful. That hair, and her eyes. She has incredible legs. Once you gave a sermon on forgiveness. That's why, you know. Because I knew you were speaking to your wife. And I had seen your wife. She poured me a cup of coffee during the social hour. I mean, I wanted her to be my friend—"

"Fidelity and monogamy are not the same. The body has a mission. God knows that. Hell, a man will fuck a goat."

"Fine," she said, teasing him. "So I'm a goat?"

"That's not what I mean. You shouldn't cheat like that in conversation."

"Last week, on the Nature Channel, I swear to God I saw two rhinos humping the same cow. On the Serengeti or someplace. These rhino studs, there they go, back to back. It's not the erection that bothers me, or what one even does with it. It's just not knowing."

"How do you know he's leaving you?"

"Oh God, David. The guilt! If he loves me, and I know he does, he cannot want to hurt me."

"Maybe—"

"No. He's going to leave me. Did you know the penis of a rhinoceros weighs fifty-seven pounds? He's going to leave me because he does not want to have a child. Because he doesn't want to have to worry about anybody but himself. He's going to leave me because were the sexes reversed, it's exactly what I would do right now to him."

The next day she was off and did not go in to the hospital, and that night she ate dinner with a friend, Jacqueline, who lived down the street. They met at a restaurant in Tempe. To get there, Susie had to drive past the university. She drove past A Mountain—the small hill tucked behind the stadium branded with the university's crimson initial, *A*. Sometimes she would hike the mountain with her friend, Jacqueline, who was married fairly recently. Jacqueline had broken off a six-year love affair with a woman before falling in love with her new husband. Susie thought about that, driving past the mountain, loving another woman. Certainly she'd had her various opportunities. At the same time, she loved the man whom she'd seduced at the age of seventeen.

He was recently divorced, a friend of her father's. He spent two weeks in their home in Paradise Valley. At night, after taking a shower, she would walk by the guest room wearing a T-shirt. Her hair was always wet; she remembered that. She would stop by his bedroom, just to say hello, and then one morning her father scolded her, and she went off to school. That afternoon she cut her classes and, while her father was still at work, returned home early.

The man, her father's guest, was in the den, reading the *Wall Street Journal*.

She said, "I am going to make you fall in love with me, whether you like it or not. My father will be angry."

She turned on her heel, which she had seen Ann-Margret do in a movie, and went out to the pool. There she removed her Catholic school clothes—white blouse, plaid skirt, knee socks—and leapt into the pool. After a while, he stepped out onto the Kool Deck. He said, "I'm thirty-four. Which is handsome now. But it won't be in ten years. A man my age only disintegrates."

"Beauty," she called from the pool, treading water, "is skin deep."

"You're going to Harvard? Next year?"

"Yes."

"I will be living in Boston. Maybe we can have dinner sometime."

And that is how she knew she had not been mistaken, because despite the nervousness in his voice, the obvious and self-asserted erection beneath his trousers, he instead turned and went into the house, where he called her father to explain he would be dropping by his office in a very short while.

In college she dated boys, and a professor, and almost a Caribbean woman who lived across the hall her sophomore year until the girl was suddenly deported for drug smuggling. Eventually Susie began seeing regularly the man who would become her husband, and they married. For the ceremony, she wore a dress by Vera Wang, and her father, not knowing what to give the couple, bought them a Chagall he thought particularly cheerful and optimistic. They spent their first two years together in Vienna, another three in Manhattan. Then they came to Phoenix, city of the flaming bird, rising from the ashes of modernity and a couple hundred thousand parking lots. They made their friends. They passed their lives.

A road to heaven took you to a place, preferably home. She called her answering machine from the restaurant. There was a message from her husband. By the sound of it, he was sorry to have missed her previous call. He explained he would be taking the London flight to Phoenix. He explained enough was enough. She could return to Italy with him, and then on to Paris, or he could cancel the trip. He had already canceled Bangkok, he said. He'd been doing a lot of thinking, he said. He wanted to build a nursery.

She was crying. She replayed the message, just to hear his voice. All around her, well-dressed married men from the bar kept their eyes peeled. She thought about adultery, and the men in the bar, checking out the women, as if the act of it had actually become a fashion symbol among the up and coming. She thought about her husband, who would arrive dehydrated from the flight. He would be jet-lagged for days and sleep like the dead. Happy endings, she thought. Happy endings weren't supposed to be permitted, and she understood this was not an ending, but rather just another beginning—a rocket, entering another stage, adjusting to its new orbit around the center of their lives.

The heart of the matter, her husband would say, falling into their bed.

She returned to her table, and Jacqueline looked surprised and happy at the same time. Later they parted company and Susie drove to a bookstore. Inside there were people reading magazines. She wandered to the back and found the fiction and plucked from the shelf a hardcover copy of *Master and Commander*. She stood in line behind a half dozen people purchasing compact discs and calendars. One woman was buying several copies of *Vogue*. The cover featured a dress by Versace, the Kingpin of Slut.

"I love him," said the bookseller, ringing up her purchase. "Did you find everything all right?"

She wanted to say, Why do you ask?

She thought, Why does anybody ask anything of anybody?

She thought about her husband reading a novel on an airplane while crossing the Atlantic. The heart, she thought, is an open book; it wants only to be read. Her husband would be arriving in Phoenix at nearly the same time of his departure from London. So where did the time go? In the parking lot, where it had begun to rain, she located her car while the air filled deliciously with mesquite. Twenty minutes later, she arrived at the hospital.

The lights to the room were off, the room lit up by the city lights. The boy was gazing at the ceiling, his face riven in agony. A dish of melted strawberry ice cream sat beside his nightstand.

She knocked gently. At first he didn't recognize her without her lab coat. Her dress was damp from the rain, like her hair. He wiped the back of his hand across his eyes.

"Hi," he said.

"Tomorrow's the big day."

"They gave me something," he said. "To help me sleep. But I can't sleep. Just dopey."

She thought about her husband, who for many years simply could not fall asleep without first ejaculating. She said, stepping closer, "I brought you a book, for after. If you like it we can get the rest. There are a dozen more. Lots of sea air."

He said, brightening, "Thank you."

It was then she realized his sheet was twisted at his ankles. He was naked, had obviously been inspecting the damage. She said, reaching for the sheet, "Aren't you cold?"

"It itches," he said. "I can't scratch."

She thought, How quickly shame escapes. She said, "That means you're healing."

"It itches," he said. "Like before."

"Soon," she said, which is what she always said. "Soon. Life is long."

She drew the sheet up toward his thighs. He was crying again—exhaling, inhaling.

"It was my dad," he said. "Not me."

"Your dad?"

"I was in the garage. And he came home early. They'd sent him home for drinking. And he came into the garage, and I had all this gas over me. I was scrubbing it, you know, to kill the crabs. I read that if you don't get rid of them you can give them to your family."

"It's okay," she said. "And it's easy to catch. Really."

"I never did it, you know. Not properly. I went to this strip joint, just to *look*. And this lady kept touching me. She, you know, she kept doing that, and I knew it was wrong to have them. And my dad, he sees me with no clothes on in the garage by his tools and blows his top. He starts calling me faggot and candy ass and then he pulls out a cigarette. And then he says, *Here, I'll kill the critters.*"

She gazed out the window overlooking the Valley of the Sun.

"He used a match," the boy said. "Everybody thinks I did it."

She felt his hand, first on her arm. She turned, and smiled. He was gazing at her body. He could see the nipples of her breasts, she knew that, taut from the rain and now chill air. He brought his hand to her waist.

"You're so beautiful," he said.

She took his hand and held it close. She could feel her heart beating wildly. He was struggling now to lift his face to kiss her.

So why, she thought, does she love her husband? *Because I can.* She said, more sharply than she'd intended, "No."

The boy fell back as if slapped.

"It's a body," she said, stepping back. "This is my body. And that is your body. You must not fall in love with me, because my heart belongs to my husband, whom I love." She said, stepping closer to him, "You don't believe this, but someday you are going to fall in love properly. And she will love you more than you can bear. She will love you to the grave."

"I can't, you know—"

"You have your eyes. You have your mind and a good, strong heart. The body is not the essence. It's what protects that essence, so you can keep it safe. So you can nourish it and give it back to others."

He said, "I love you, Susie."

"And you will love another," she said. "And then another, perhaps at the same time, which will make your life complicated and rich."

"I want—"

"Shhh," she said, letting go. She said, receding further from his view, and making him a promise, "Sleep, and tomorrow you will wake."

So why do you ask?

That night, before she went to sleep, she kicked off her

shoes and opened up a bottle of wine. It was red wine—a burgundy, her husband would say, with body. She put music on the stereo and raised all the blinds to her house. She drank a glass of wine, and then another. At times, when the music was particularly moving, she danced by herself in the living room. By the third glass, she had begun a conversation with her husband, who was flying somewhere overhead, and then she started a conversation with David, who was lying in bed beside his sleeping wife. You don't understand, she explained to David. *She's sound asleep!* Then she had another glass of wine. The wine, if one tried hard enough, could taste like blood, like the iron which informs the bloodstream, and which at certain times became the Son of God. Frankly she was used to the smell of blood; it caused her to feel at home and grateful for the dirt below it. She stepped out into the yard, the dust beneath her toes, the music pumping into the night, and admonished the half-moon sailing across the sky to travel safely. In the morning she would greet her husband at a place called Sky Harbor International. Without even knowing it her husband had become a ward of the sky. She said, setting down her wine, preparing to make a point, that a boy should not have to burn in hell. A boy should burn instead inside the body of his beloved.

In the reflection of the windows to her house, the house she had made together with her husband, she saw herself clearly in the half-light of the moon. The floodlights streaming across the desert landscaping—everywhere the plants had been selected to grow and prosper in the desert sunlight, each according to its means. An ocotillo here: there, across the light of the pool, a thriving ironwood. The plants had been given root by the seeds from which they sprang. Last spring the boy's father had lit a match in order to set his son on fire. She watched him now, the boy, rolling on the ground, putting out the flames. She watched him reach for cover. And just where did one keep a blanket inside a man's garage? Maybe a pup tent or a drop cloth. Had she been there, she knew what she would do. Had she been there she would have used her dress, and she removed it now, beneath the sky, before the image of herself removing her dress beneath the sky.

She kicked off her underwear. She removed the comb from her hair.

It's a body, she had said to the boy.

She stood before the windows to her house, holding the fabric of her dress before her, trying it on for size.

Now you see it, she could have said. Now you don't.

THE GATEWAY

Home is where one starts from.
—T. S. ELIOT

B eat, they say in the screenplay trade—not to indicate violence, or the plausibility of victory, or defeat. When we say beat we mean instead *the passage of time.*

A moment, say. Preferably one meant to be felt, like life.

I was in Paris, staying at a hotel behind the Cathedral St. Sulpice, when I was visited by an old girlfriend. I was sitting naked on the bed, a white cotton spread, fresh from the bath because earlier that morning I had been caught in the rain. There was rain falling in the courtyard filled with flowers. My wife, Phoebe, was out shopping for a new Parisian hat for our three-year-old daughter. She wanted me to buy a new suit.

We're in Paris, she said. Buy yourself a suit.

On the way to the Arc de Triomphe, Phoebe had discovered a designer she instantly took a shine to. On the way back to our hotel we stopped again and she purchased three new dresses and was, my guess, feeling slightly spendthrift. In the small, polished store I held Isolde on my hip and watched my wife through the slightly parted fabric of the changing room slip her body into one dress, and then another; I watched her pull back her hair only to let it alight upon her long, pale neck. Fabulous, said the woman who ran the boutique, standing beside me, lifting her chin and watching my wife. The woman turned to me and said, in that oddly intimate moment, You have a beautiful family, and then the woman reached for my daughter to brush aside a lock of her hair. Then my wife stepped out of the dressing room in this mid-thigh silk dress, the color of a robin's egg, or the St. Louis sky in spring. The dress had spaghetti straps and a row of buttons running from the center of my wife's chest, down across her navel to the hemline, and I thought, This is the woman with whom I have made it all the way to Paris.

There was also a raw silk shawl, which covered her bare shoulders. We had a daughter now, Isolde. We had a house on San Bonita in St. Louis with a Stickley-influenced banister and a seventy-year-old oak staircase—original stained glass windows, a slate roof over our heads. The person whom you marry, it changes your life.

And the person whom you do not marry?

Earlier, while Phoebe and Isolde went shopping for a hat, I had sat in the rainy mist in a park across from Notre Dame. I was sitting there, smoking a Gauloise, when I realized a hundred feet off to my left there was a pair of lovers on a bench, beneath a handsome tree, which protected them from the drizzling rain. The woman had her raincoat spread about her boyfriend's hips, straddling him in the rain, and I could hear them laughing, because naturally they must have been in love. I picked myself up, moved to another bench, and then it really began to rain and I gave in to the weather and walked back to the hotel. On the way back, I stopped in at the Cathedral St. Sulpice to light a candle for my father, who had recently died, and to give thanks—I don't know to whom—for the fact of my wife and daughter.

Back in my room, I ordered hot chocolate and took a bath. I opened the window to smoke a cigarette, and sat on the bed, listening to the rain, and turned on CNN, World Edition, and there she was—Amanda Cunningham Amachi. The girl I met in college. The girl I lived with in California while writing screenplays. The girl who gave me lice. The girl who after telling me she was pregnant then proceeded to have an abortion, without telling me, and prevented me from becoming a father sooner than I ever should have. The girl who told me, after I decided to give up on Hollywood, Oh God, Thomas. I always knew you were a failure.

I met Ed Zwick once. The director? That's another story.

My wife had lived in Paris for a year and a half after she finished college—painting pictures—while I was pitching scripts in L.A. My thinking was I'd sell out to Hollywood in order later to write haunting novels about the human condition. When that fell apart, I started writing nonunion scripts for children's television at nine hundred dollars a whack. To get by, I had to sell two a month, which meant I actually had to write five. If you know anything about Hollywood, then you know that children's television is the scut work of the industry, and if you have children, you may have seen one or two of my episodes, like "Dildar and the Laser of Doom." Lots of kung fu and galactic monsters and neon outfits with invasive special effects. The week I finally realized I should be ashamed, I returned alone to St. Louis—the place of my birth, the very Gateway to the West. The French, they discovered St. Louis. By 1904 it had become one of the most industrial and economically driven cities of the world.

Amanda Cunningham Amachi—I'd known her before the Amachi became appended—was living in a small town north of Dubuque, Iowa. She was an associate director of economic development. She had gained weight and, having married my former roommate from college, Dan Amachi, had now brought forth into this world two children. He was, last I'd heard, regional sales manager for Briggs & Stratton—the engine on your lawnmower. Apparently, the small town in which they had settled had missed out on the economic boom of the nineties, its downtown having been decimated by the encroaching Wal-Marts and Home Depots, and Amanda Cunningham Amachi, as associate director of economic development for the city council of Three Falls, had been called upon by CNN to serve as an expert witness.

First I left Hollywood, land of the movie house, and then I went home, and now I sell people houses and make dreams come true. I sell houses in the suburbs of Kirkwood and Webster Groves and, if a client really has some dough, Clayton. I generally don't sell the city, because the city is destroyed, we actually have abandoned skyscrapers, and you can buy a house in St. Louis on your credit card, but I do sell a lot of houses and I have a lot of people now who sell houses for me. I'll show you a house in University City if I know you don't have any kids, same with the Central West End, but if you do have kids, and unless I know you are prepared to give up your lease payments on your SUV and instead spend your money on private schools, then I know you aren't going to buy a house there, because I'm the guy who also listens to your concerns about the schools. I'm the guy who explains to first-time buyers the meaning of points and listens patiently while you talk yourself into spending more than you thought you could possibly afford in spite of your lease payments on that SUV. I'm the guy who, along with another at Saint Louis University, started a housing program for refugees across the world. And before that, I was also the guy who used to teach Advanced Screenwriting for Hollywood as a part-time professional at a local university which fancies itself as being its own world headquarters. Honest, that's what the sign says, complete with a picture of the globe.

World Headquarters.

After I failed big in Hollywood, I got in my old car and drove across the country. Once I hit the city limits, I went directly to the arch. I put my hand upon the sleek and silver curve of it and the world went right on by. A couple hundred years ago, the French, they wanted to make some discoveries, which is what travel always permits, so they came to America. When I went to Paris, I flirted with a woman with whom my wife would select three dresses. The woman wore stylish eyeglasses, and when the French arrived in what would eventually become New Orleans, they wandered up the Mississippi River to Laclede's Landing and built the once magnificent city of St. Louis. They built the city into which I was born and took their fill.

On Art Hill, in Forest Park, there is a magnificent statue of Mr. St. Louis, overlooking the park, which is designed to resemble those in Paris. When I was a kid, we used to steal his sword.

As Sean Connery says to Julia Ormond, *Marry the king, Guinevere. But love the man.*

Years ago, when my wife was in Paris, she was twenty-two and living in the Seventh Arrondissement. Her boyfriend back in the States, Future Rock Star, was sleeping with a woman who also had a crush on Phoebe and who would later become an editorial lieutenant of a magazine empire. My wife did not know Claire was sleeping with Future Rock Star. She thought they were having coffee in Boston. I know because she was writing to him at that very same moment that I was standing in St. Louis with my hand on the tender curve of the Gateway Arch. All of this is true.

When you visit, Phoebe wrote, *we'll make love in the Luxembourg Gardens.*

There was a boy, Jean Claude, who lived in the flat across the hall. Jean Claude was beautiful and shy, and on one fine spring day when Phoebe's toilet backed up, he opened the door for her at her knock.

Yes? said Jean Claude.

My toilet backed up, Phoebe said. May I use yours?

She was giddy with the excuse to step inside his living room, which was filled with books. The terror of living in a beautiful place like Paris is that you are always lonely, no matter how many people you might sleep with. What you want is someone to hold your hand. What you want is somebody to look into your eyes and explain that the ache and absolute apprehension you feel inside your heart is normal. Life is bitter. Life is sweet. Let's talk, then we'll fuck.

The landlord charged my wife several thousand francs for breaking the toilet. It was one of those space-saving European metal things which always cause the room to smell like piss. My wife, she stepped into Jean Claude's bathroom, and then she washed her hands, which were stained with paint and smelled faintly of turpentine, and then her face. She thought, I am in Paris in a French boy's bathroom. There were condoms on the sink. She stepped out of the bathroom, water on her cheeks, as if she had been crying, and Jean Claude handed her a glass of wine. His eyeglasses were slightly smudged and the hair on his wrist was fine and pale. He handed her a glass of red wine and said, Phoebe?

Yes, she said, her heart lifting.

He raised a finger into the air and touched the mole on the edge of her mouth. Phoebe, he said. That means *moon*, no?

Yes, Phoebe said. She began to unbutton her blouse, which was covered with paint, then hesitated. Catching his eye, she began again, and said, Want to see?

Jean Claude kissed her hands. From the feel of things, he had an enormous penis. They could hear Rosalia, another tenant, across the hall. Apparently Rosalia had lost her keys. Phoebe ripped open her jeans, and then his. She kicked off her shoes. Additionally, this was Phoebe's first uncircumcised penis, which amazed her, the way it emerged so keenly from the flesh which held it. Paris was a boy, too, she thought. Paris was

the boy who stole Helen of Troy and, in turn, started the entire
Trojan War. She slipped the condom on Jean Claude tenderly.

It was a tight fit. For a while he hurt inside of her, but after
a while the hurt turned to a kind of sweet and rueful pleasure. When she was three, she had seen her father naked, once,
though she no longer remembered it. A man has a son, the
world pivots on its axis; but when a man has a daughter, a little
girl like my own, even the axis turns. It turns on the very center of your heart. Then the condom split. That night, return-
ing to her flat, the smell of sex in her hair, which reminded her
of freshly mown grass, Phoebe wrote to her boyfriend, Future
Rock Star, who was at that moment having an argument with
a future editorial lieutenant. For the second time that evening,
Phoebe removed her jeans, and then her underwear and socks,
while I went to my father's house and sat in the kitchen, drinking a beer, and explained to him my decision to give up on
Hollywood. Everybody has to eat, I said, making excuses for
what I'd done. I don't remember what he said, but I do remember my father pouring himself a beer and nodding sympathet-
ically, taking his time, not wanting to raise a head. And years
later, sitting naked in my hotel room behind the Cathedral
St. Sulpice, before the open window which looked out onto a
courtyard filled with flowers, I watched Phoebe sit at her small
table in her small flat. I watched her cross her legs and take out
a tablet of purple paper on which to write her boyfriend back
in the States a love letter. I watched the ink from her pen, following the direction of her mind, her tongue and her breath.

I've met the sweetest boy, she wrote. *He works for the tele-*

phone company part time and studies Philosophy. She wrote, *Give Claire my love.*

She wrote, *Watch out for the groupies.*

She used a lot of Xs and Os—*kisses & hugs.* She kissed the paper, her lips tasting the faintest trace of the tree from which it once came, and the bitter scent of ink, and then she went to bed and dreamed of home, which was far away, all the way across the Atlantic. She fell asleep along the way at sea.

Ron Shelton, too. I met him once, and he was kind and polite, and he insisted I send him something, but I never did. I liked leaving L.A. with an open invitation like that.

Meet me for coffee? said the woman, slipping me a piece of paper, on which she had written her telephone number and the name of a café. Phoebe and Isolde were outside, on the Parisian sidewalk, looking for puddles. The woman had fine hair parted in the center and a silk blouse through which I could see the fabric of her lingerie. I signed the credit card receipt, and slid it back across the counter, and then her wedding-ringed hand fell onto mine, and I said, I've never been to Paris.

It's lovely in the spring, said the woman. I do not live far from here.

She stepped back, and laughed, and glanced at a co-worker, equally chic, stepping through the curtains. The woman before me with the rich perfume wiped her mouth with the back of her hand and said, Five o'clock? I will show you some sights.

This is not the kind of thing which often happens to single

men, or rather it does, but only on the late-night cable with all the rented furniture. Like crack cocaine and unfettered capitalism, like wars of aggression, it's the kind of thing which destroys a home, which is what you dream of most when you do not have one. Home ownership. It's why we privilege the industry with our tax laws and it's why we have ancillary industries with patriotic names to furnish them—Ethan Allen, Martha Stewart. It's why, after you fail at one career, you can always take up selling houses. When you walk inside somebody's house, you can tell how much they read. You get instantly a feel for their sex life by the size of the television in the bedroom and the pictures on the walls, the pillows on the bed and the color of the sheets. Is there a copy of the *Kama Sutra* on the nightstand? In the kitchen, you can spot instantly who knows how to cook. My father, who died three weeks before my seventh anniversary, used to say he liked Amanda Cunningham because, as he put it, she was corn-fed.

Though I was in Paris, sitting in a park in the rain beside a pair of lovers, smoking a Gauloise across from Notre Dame, I had been feeling sad. There were boughs protecting the lovers from the rain. My father was a great thinker. The Colossus, his colleagues called him. My father, who worked with seeds, invented a process which led various industries to develop agricultural forms of genetic engineering. In the pictures I have of myself in my youth, you can see I am my father's son. I am my father's son *sans* the colossal intellect.

Earlier that day, in our perfect hotel, I'd had breakfast—a bowlful of coffee, chocolate croissants—beneath a glass canopy, and Michelle, the waitress and chambermaid and sometimes desk clerk, cooed over Isolde and brought her apricots. While Phoebe read her share of the *Herald Tribune*, I read a story about genetic engineering. The French agricultural community was very upset about it. One leader, Mr. French Leader of the Free Farms, was quoted as saying, *These huge tomatoes. It is so American. It is an outrage and an invasion just like Normandy!*

My father had been a part of that invasion. He served as a medic, tying up the various limbs which might not need to be completely severed, on the way to liberating Paris. He finished college on the GI Bill and became a genius, and I know for a fact my father didn't want to make fake food: he wanted instead to feed the world. The starving kids in Ethiopia and El Salvador and China—it's one thing to make a life, but quite another to feed it. He'd say, Whatever you do, Thomas, make this world a better place.

I was sad because the world was full of such sweetness and mercy and light and because I wanted to be at least partially responsible for some of it. Phoebe says she was a good enough artist to know she herself never would be a good one, which is why she now runs a gallery. It's her fate, she'll tell a young artist she wants to show, to help the other. And besides, she *wants* to.

Man, says Aristotle, is desire. The best I can explain is this:

Once upon a time, a boy named Paris desired a pretty girl, and in so doing started a war which became an epic poem and then a city to which I took my wife and our three-year-old daughter to celebrate our seventh anniversary and the fact of our lives together. In the park across from Notre Dame, two lovers were making love, and possibly a baby, in the rain. My old girlfriend was on the television. After she became pregnant, she told me so in the kitchen of our apartment, and I said, This complicates things, but we can work it out, can't we? And then Amanda Cunningham said she wasn't certain, but that she was very glad I was not upset with her, and she said she also wasn't sure she wanted to spend the rest of her life with me, and then she went to a friend's house for the weekend, just to take a break, she said, during which her friend took her to a clinic where she held Amanda's hand while a doctor in fresh scrubs performed the generally uncomplicated procedure. Meanwhile, there she was on the television in Paris, and a married woman in a tony boutique had slipped to me a piece of paper asking for a date, paper which smelled like her rich perfume, having been in contact with her wrist, and now my wife, Phoebe, was shopping for a hat on the Champs Elysées and Isolde, our daughter, was holding her mother's hand. Isolde was holding her mother's hand tightly because she liked the way her mother's wedding ring made a grip for her small fingers. And Henri, the concierge at our perfect hotel, was ringing up his niece because, as he was about to explain, the American couple with the sweet little girl wanted a sitter for tonight to celebrate.

What I love most about the history of the world is the history of the world—yours, mine, a pale woman with a perfumed wrist who slips you a piece of paper across a countertop. And what I love about that stranger is that brief moment of contact, that moment of possibility when, you never know, another world just might be opening up its doors to welcome you inside.

Do you stay? Or do you go?

I love the word *stay*—the action of halting, or a corset stiffened with bones. To fasten. More at *stand*. I love the way my wife's body fills a dress.

All of this is true. Years ago, at a swishy private college in New England, Phoebe did her senior thesis on Sir Thomas Malory's *Le Morte d'Arthur,* which is, among other things, the story of King Arthur and Lancelot and Guinevere. And even more years ago, at a slightly less swishy private college in Minnesota, I did the same thing. Given that less than one-half of 1 percent of the entire country has even *read Le Morte d'Arthur,* it seemed like fate, us bumping into each other like this, in the French Quarter of St. Louis, Soulard, before a row house I had recently renovated and carved into three apartments. I gave Phoebe a break on the rent and installed for her a security system. She was this long-legged, pale girl in sandals and jeans and a tank—dark hair; a long, pale neck; Mediterranean eyes. She had a beauty mark on the corner of her mouth. I warned her to be careful with her sandals, lest she step on an abandoned hypodermic. I asked her if she had seen the arch. I said that to really see the arch, first you had to touch it. I asked her if she'd like to go to the symphony.

Yes, she said.

I mean with me. Would you like to go with me?

Most girls you meet in St. Louis, they want to go to a disco named Oz, across the river to all the legalized vice, so when

Phoebe said, Yes, that would be nice, my heart trilled. Then I dated her in courtly fashion for a period of several months. I remember the first time we kissed, on the steps of her apartment, the scent of wine on her breath. I remember her explaining to me that a man she knew at Harvard Business School, future Internet billionaire, had asked her to come back to Cambridge and marry him, and I remember her saying, squeezing my hand, I'm not going to, don't worry, and then she stepped inside the door and shut it gently behind her and I listened to her feet climb the stairs I had spent two weeks sanding and then refinishing on my hands and knees. It was a beautiful night, and I returned to my car and drove to my own then house on Lafayette which was kitty-corner to the Abandoned City Hospital. I sat on the porch with my friend, Benjamin, a cop who had been shot two years ago by a fellow officer. The copper and wiring and fixtures had long been stripped out of the Abandoned City Hospital. Benjamin told me stories about how black kids who were shot didn't get CPR. He told me he was thinking of moving to Chicago, or San Francisco, or reenlisting. I had met Benjamin after being mugged, when he had come over to the hospital to take my report, and then he had taken my screenplay writing course, at World Headquarters University, because as an African-American cop he wanted to set the record straight, but actually he just wanted to meet some girls. Mostly he wrote screenplays about a cop who wrote screenplays who just wanted to meet some girls, and then I quit teaching Advanced Screenplay Writing for Hollywood, because I had no business doing that, and he quit writing screenplays, not having met any girls, and that night Benjamin asked me if I was getting any, meaning the regular thing it means, and then we drank a couple beers and listened to the gunfire in our neighborhood. Earlier that week our neighbor, Christopher, had been shot in the thigh for his wallet, and a week before a retired school teacher had been raped in Lafayette Park while taking her morning walk. Beside the Abandoned City Hospital there were drug dealers on the corner making deals. Then Benjamin, being off-duty, called his precinct to request a show of the flag.

My last screenplay for children's television was about a giant crab with lasers that threatened to destroy Civilization as We Know It.

The episode was called, "Civilization as We Know It."

I was named after a poet raised in St. Louis who once wrote, In my beginning is my end.

Phoebe was lonely in Paris, writing letters to her boyfriend, who was sleeping with her best friend; she was lonely in Paris and painting nude portraits of Jean Claude. After their initial introduction to each other's physiognomy, during which Jean Claude had come in her hair, she had asked him to sit for her, on the rooftop of their building, where she often worked. In the background of one picture, she has drawn the silhouette of the Eiffel Tower. Then Jean Claude took a photograph which hangs today in Phoebe's study: she is twenty-two and long-legged, wearing a short skirt, straddling the Eiffel Tower which appears in the distant background. You cannot see her face, but Phoebe tells me she was happy at the moment.

Jean Claude was flattered. Sometimes he wore rollerblades

and would skate around the rooftop. There was a garden filled with flowers and herbs. Phoebe began sunbathing on the roof, the springtime sun warming her long body, while Jean Claude practiced his saxophone. They would skate together through the streets of Paris. They drank espresso in the cafés. Phoebe wrote her parents and thanked them for providing her with the time of her life, which is what all parents provide—the time of your life. As Patrick Swayze says in *Dirty Dancing* to Baby, placing her hand against his chest, *Thump thump.*

My father died on a Sunday afternoon, in his big car, backing out of the driveway. He had been to church—St. George's—and had come home for a quick lunch, and had gathered some notebooks in order to start work on a new project involving pumpkin seeds. After he had placed the transmission of his car into reverse, the heart attack struck—the iced pain in the chest, as if he had just swallowed a snowball; the ache of the bone-cold numbness in his arm, and then shoulder. He died fairly swiftly, his foot slipping off the brake, permitting the car's idling engine to roll the vehicle back down the drive, and then left, toward the Dubinkerrs', where he rolled up onto the front lawn. The grass needed cutting. I had sold the Dubinkerrs their house two years earlier—a typical U City three-story made of fine St. Louis brick, designed specifically for the faculty and deans at Washington University. The Dubinkerrs had two Asian girls they had adopted, and as my father's car rolled up onto their lawn, the philosophy professor, Dr. Dubinkerr, yelled to his little girls to stand back. Stand Back! he yelled, spreading wide his arms by which to shield them. They had been playing Tea Time with dolls and a china tea set. The pro-

fessor ran to my father's car, and pulled him out, and he began to perform CPR, his breath spilling into my father's now
deflated chest. He called to his wife, also Professor Dubinkerr,
who was presently reading a set of exams on modern political
theory—Locke, Hobbes, A Great Big Fish. And then she heard
her husband's cry, and the cry of her daughters, Amber and
Kaitlin, each of whom came running through the house into
the kitchen, screaming.

Mommy, Kaitlin exclaimed. Daddy's kissing Mr. Sellers!

The Scientist, Amber said, nodding. He's on the grass.

The ambulance took forty-five minutes to arrive, because
there had been a gang-related shoot-out on Delmar, two officers down, and there was a little boy down, too, who died en
route having had a bullet pierce his liver. By the time the ambulance arrived to rescue my father, the one Professor Dubinkerr
was putting down her girls for a nap, and the other was drinking a glass of lemonade to get the taste of my father's quick
lunch—pastrami and muenster—out of his mouth. At the fu-
neral, they each wore black, and later the Professors Dubinkerr
gave to me a signed edition of *On Death and Dying*, which had
been inscribed with best wishes to a woman named Jean.

I found on my father's desk a letter he had been writing to
me. It was a letter to celebrate my forthcoming seventh anniversary, and he had placed beside it three tickets to Paris. He
wrote, among other things, that the best thing I ever did was
marry Phoebe.

Take your family to Paris now, he wrote, *and you will be able
to return. I regret I never took you there myself. Your loving father, Dad.*

This is what my father thought when he was dying:
God, it hurts.

If the cell is the source of life, as my father used to say, then we are bound to be prisoners of our condition. When I was writing my children's television screenplays, I was always given an assignment—namely, the special effects footage with the karate kids in masked outfits, fighting the various and mechanized demonic beasts, all of which had been shot in Japan. My job was to take the Child American Actors and the Special Effects and to join them by way of a plot kids could sit through—the brain-candy of death and destruction and doom. One kid, Alexander Jay Pratt, had a mother who thought Handsome Alexander should be earning a whole lot more, and so I wrote also the episode which made Alexander Jay Pratt—the kid in green—a Senator for Galactic Peace and sent him through the Great Portal to the Great Galactic Peace Conference in the Sky. A new kid in green was on board the very next episode. It was magic. Better yet, it was non–capital intensive and highly profitable. It was the kind of magic only a tightwad Hollywood producer would ever dream up, and it made my heart ache. There was enough violence in the world without my encouraging four-year-olds to kick each other in the face.

Phoebe was in love, and in Paris, but still she was feeling lonely. Meanwhile, her Future Rock Star boyfriend had by now cut an album, and Claire had written to Phoebe an awkward letter in which Claire confessed her deepest longing thus:

> *Remember when we went skinny-dipping in*
> *the lake? Remember the way I looked at you,*

and my chest flushed, and then I ran into the
lake? I have become lovers with your lover so
that I may become your own. Please, Claire
wrote, *please do not be angry with him. He is a*
dog, like all men.

She wrote, *I love you and want you to want*
me to come to Paris. A rose is a rose—will you
be my Alice?—is a rose.

Phoebe loved flowers—and still does—and she read that
letter on the garden terrace, at night, the scent of freesias and
lilies and springtime roses filling up the night. Behind her rose
the Eiffel Tower, that mechanized hymn to phallic torture,
glowering in the night sky, all rivets and bolts. She thought it
odd the way the French felt compelled to light it up at night,
which struck her as faintly impolite, like shining a flashlight
on your lover in the dark. She lit a cigarette, being in Paris, and
then she held the letter before her and set it on fire.

You light up my life, she thought, which was once the title
of a pop song, as well as a made-for-television movie.

Dust to dust. She brushed the ashes from her fingertips,
and lap, and then she wiped her fingertips along the legs of
her jeans. She reached for her Evian, and took a drink, and
then she set the Evian aside, and went down the spiral case to
her room, where she poured herself a monstrous glass of wine.
Then she poured herself another. Then she grabbed her wallet
and her black leather jacket and went out for the night.

She walked to St. Michel, and stopped at a café, and ordered Pernod. There was an American couple nearby, bicker-
ing, and then she went to a bar which played salsa music on the

stereo and served Jack Daniels in thick-bottomed glasses, and she drank that, neat, one after the other. A boy approached—wispy-bearded, cigarette in hand—and asked her if she'd like to get it on. Hey Baby, said the boy. He kissed her cheek and nudged himself into her body. She could feel his cock rubbing against her thigh, and then he kissed her again.

In France, to kiss can often be to fuck. *Baiser.* She said, kissing him, Let's dance. She said, taking his hand, I might be a lesbian before you know it.

This caused the boy some excitement. There were two women dancing together, and there was Phoebe, drinking her bourbon, and now the French boy who wanted to get it on. He looked like a biker—black jeans, black leather jacket, just like hers—who did not know how to ride a motorbike. He looked like any other boy who lived in Paris.

He said, *Je m'appelle Louis,* and she said, *Ah oui, Louis. Enchantée, Louis.* She said, A lesbian does not sleep with the man she loves.

The room was smoky, lit with candles, and Louis was grabbing at her breasts. She thought about going home with him, almost glancingly, but she simply couldn't get that far in her mind. Instead she understood finally what she had always feared most. The thought struck clean as the light of day, or a knife.

I will never be a decent painter, she thought. Fuck it.

To avoid breaking into tears, she went to the bar, and had another fast drink, and then she left. Outside she blinked her eyes into the hysteria of the city lights. She walked along the streets. Once, at Pigalle, she had gone into a dark theatre with Jean Claude to see a sex show where a man in charge of special effects had pinched her ass. She had also spent a lot of time at the Louvre. She walked by Napoléon's cannons. She pictured Rodin, sculpting his naked bodies out of marble, and then breathing into them a life of their own, before fucking his sitter, and then having a bottle of wine to celebrate his life's work. Everywhere you went, Paris was full of itself.

By now she was stumbling, and weeping, and she discovered along the way that she had lost somewhere along the way her black leather jacket. Eventually she found a cab, and the driver asked her if she needed to go to the hospital, and she said, No, only to my flat. I'm lost.

We are all lost, he said. You want to buy some cocaine? Some Ecstasy?

She said, Take me to the Seventh.

On the stairs to her flat, she twice stumbled, and by the time she got there, she wasn't certain whose door she belonged to. She stood in front of her door and thought, If you go in there, you just might disappear.

Who am I, she thought. And why?

Paris is an existential city. She had left her keys inside her flat, beside her hot water pot, on the tea bag box. She turned and banged on Jean Claude's room, in case he might be home, though she knew he wouldn't be. To be, she thought, is to do. She walked down the hall to Rosalia's room. She banged at the door. There was music, Bryan Ferry, the kind of music one had sex to, and she turned, and Rosalia opened the door, wearing an unbuttoned shirt, a blue denim shirt which belonged to Jean Claude—Phoebe knew because Phoebe had worn that very same shirt on like occasions—and Rosalia said, her mouth flushed, Phoebe! and Phoebe put her arms inside of Rosalia's open shirt, onto Rosalia's waist, and kissed her deeply on the mouth to see what it would taste like, which wasn't much different from kissing Jean Claude, or her Future Rock Star boyfriend back in the States, except maybe for the lack of beard, and then Jean Claude, sitting naked on the futon, beside his sax, said, Phoebe?

Breast to robin-hearted breast. Rosalia stepped back into the room. Phoebe, she said, taking Phoebe's hands with her own. This—this is just friendship. It is—

Though she knew that, now, and never before in her entire life had she ever felt so entirely alone. So profoundly discrete and disconnected. She felt utterly at a loss, a leaf tossed into the self-important Parisian breeze, and then she rushed past Rosalia, and ducked into the bathroom, and vomited.

Later, she rinsed her mouth and took a bath, in the foot of Rosalia's shower, the water pouring down upon her. Jean Claude had found his spare key to her apartment. Bryan Ferry was singing *more than this* and she sat in the foot of the bath rocking.

Rosalia loaned her a robe—a hip-length red kimono with Japanese flowers—and took her to her room and put her into bed. She brought Phoebe a glass of water. Then Phoebe, the girl who would become my wife, fell asleep beneath the comforter her mother had sent to her for Christmas. While wrapping the package for her daughter, her mother, back in Rhode

Island, had sprayed some of her own perfume on the comforter to make certain Phoebe understood just how deeply she was
loved. It smelled like home.

Later that night I was mugged on South Grand by three
kids with a chain, to whom I lost my Japanese import car and
three of my teeth. Striking me repeatedly, they cracked two
of my ribs. And later, much later, I came to realize that the
violence in my city merely mimicked the violence of the globe
and, more precisely, the terror which resides more or less within the experience of living. That is to say, some have more,
others less.

God may be omniscient, but I have never met Him. On the
seventh day, one story goes, God rested. I think during a moment when God must have blinked, or turned away to sneeze, I
think it is then my father must have died—sitting at the wheel
of his car, going backwards. I think there will never be enough
people like my father to feed the multitudes God has so neglected. Sometimes I wonder where he is, my father, and then
I understand that he is wherever it is that I happen to think
of him. My wife and I named our daughter, Isolde, after our
mutual affection for the first novel to be written in the English
language, *Le Morte d'Arthur* by Sir Thomas Malory. The root
of all romance is the story of our lives. Romance, from the
French, for *anything written in French*, and as the French will
surely tell you—especially if you are an American—that which
is novel is not always new. First Phoebe and I decided to make
our lives together, and then we decided to make our baby, and
then we decided to make love in the sunroom of our house.

This is what I was thinking about in the Luxembourg Gardens, walking along the finely graveled paths with my daughter, Isolde. She was wearing her new purple hat, her dark curly hair swaying in the breeze. She would stop at the puddles and splash in them with her red boots. We were walking by a fountain where children were sailing boats, and Phoebe was back in the hotel, planning our evening. She knew I wanted to eat in one of those restaurants Fitzgerald and Hemingway used to hang out in. She knew I was feeling rueful.

Take Isolde to the park, Phoebe said. Stop thinking so much.

At one place, a man was selling pony rides. Isolde picked out a yellow one, an old pony with a beard, and the man said, No, not him.

Why? said my daughter.

He is old, said the man. He is tired and used up.

She rode another while I sat on a bench and watched my little girl navigate the rhythms of her pony's gait. She rocked in the air and beamed in the sun like a pop song while I tapped my foot and understood I was going to have to decide what to do about that perfumed piece of paper in my pocket. At first I thought a married man does not worry about such decisions unless he is uncertain he wants to be a married man, but then I understood that this was not quite accurate, because what the body longs for is a fact, no different than the fact of an intriguing woman beckoning to you across a city park, and not an idea. A man may desire another's body, but what charges that desire is evidence of that body's spirit—in my case, the tilt of an eyebrow, or the set of her lip. The sound of her voice.

Later, while walking back to our hotel, still in the vast park, Isolde paused to examine a worm. The worm lay stranded on a patch of sand, and Isolde paused, and then she picked him up and delivered him safely to a nearby puddle.

She put together her hands and dusted them off, the way I had taught her. She said, That worm was tired and used up, too. He was old.

Like the pony, I said.

Like Grandpa Sellers, Isolde said. He's dead.

Everywhere you go, my father would say, people are dying. My father taught me that worms were necessary to fertilize the soil of the crops which grew the food we ate. My father used to say a man will sow his seeds, but a good man will do so carefully. Once, when I was a boy, my father while drinking a martini spit out an olive seed into his glass, the seed ringing against the fine glass, and I understood what he had been talking about. A good man always spits his seeds into a glass. I felt my eyes welling up, as they had been doing at the oddest moments whenever my recently dead father's presence became invoked. When my daughter was born, when my father died, I wept.

I said to Isolde, rubbing my eyes, Grandpa Sellers was old, but he's in heaven now, working in a special laboratory full of pumpkin seeds.

When you get old, Isolde said, taking my hand, you won't die. I'll protect you.

And then I scooped her up into my arms and buried my nose into her hair, which smelled like her mother's, like grass and fine soap, and she said, Like when we watch movies.

It is a sad, sweet life that I have, and what I felt, setting my daughter upon my shoulders, was gratitude for the opportunity to have it. I thought, listening to my daughter sing, Thank God Amanda Cunningham Amachi let me go twelve years ago in California.

At the time I hadn't been so certain. I had a graduate degree from one of those How to Be a Haunting Novelist programs, in which I had written seven and a half short stories, and I had by now a dozen screenplay credits for a hideous television program: I was making contacts: people said it was important to do a lot of lunch, and to get an answering machine, but my girlfriend was also sleeping with a Team Associate at the California Pizza Factory, and he was the only person who ever left a message on the new answering machine, and the smog was exacerbating my allergies, and I was also getting tired of pitching scripts about aliens: Aliens in Space, Aliens Spawning at the Wal-Mart, Aliens with Wigs in Colonial America. Everywhere I turned I saw unemployed writers and actors and singers convinced they weren't going to be the ones who remained unemployed. As Jennifer Beals dances to in *Flashdance,* Take your passion and make it happen. Most people I knew wanted to be more important than that which they did, which is the root of all failure, and then one day Amanda Cunningham came home late, smelling all damp and spoiled, and I understood, standing in our crappy, overpriced one-bedroom apartment kitchen off a Southern California freeway, that I was no better than anybody else.

Truth is, it was the first time I had failed at anything.

So I said to Amanda Cunningham, I think I'm going to call it a day and go back home. I said, testing the waters gently, Do you think you might want to come with? To which she said, *Oh God*, et cetera, and then three months later I received a postcard asking me if I'd been scratching much lately, to which I replied by telling her not to worry, it was a common ailment, lice, and that I was certain we must have picked it up mutually at the beach, and three years later I received a phone call telling me she was getting married and I said that's wonderful and she said I miss you and I said give Dan my regards and she said she would and then, that very same day I was walking through the Luxembourg Gardens with my daughter perched upon my shoulders, Amanda Cunningham Amachi had made in my hotel room various remarks about the lack of economic development in the country's heartland.

The French, they have their feelms. And we Americans our popcorn. It's a small neighborhood, what this world has become. The couple I saw in the park, making love in the rain, they weren't a handsome couple. The woman had pox scars on her face, and the man had that worn look of those who work too long outdoors for too little money which runs down their health, their life expectancy, but they were in love, at least at that moment, and the sight of them was proof of that and fortified my heart. As for Phoebe, hungover and adequately shamed by the experience of growing up, it was only a matter of time before Claire and the Future Rock Star arrived to talk things out, sensibly, which they did, each with several suitcases in tow, though by the time they landed at Charles de Gaulle

Phoebe had already returned to Rhode Island, where she spent a month walking on the beach planning her next move. She gathered her wits and took a breath and went to Manhattan and began making various contacts at the proper galleries. Claire works for a fashion magazine now, the kind in which nobody has ever suffered from acne, or pox, and the Future Rock Star is on last month's cover of a magazine. Phoebe's mother keeps tabs on this stuff, serving as an independent clipping service, sending us all the various news stories about the people Phoebe used to know.

Even in the dying city of St. Louis, with my wife and our daughter and our now forthcoming son, six months along the way, it is possible to become in the know.

Failure doesn't make for a good pitch: imagine John Nash, mad without the genius. Or the patriotic Mel Gibson without the hardy muscles. Still, I can't help it, my favorite films are those that make my heart ache. It's not the winning I admire; it's the struggle. It's the very beating of my own life's pulse.

Movies may try to capture life, but they do not replicate it. Our lives, for example, do not come supplied with a soundtrack—French horns to trumpet the American experience, catchy pop tunes to illuminate the romantic montage? The clutching of the hands, that paroxysm, at the moment of the celluloid orgasm? The art of the film is the art of illusion: first we see it through the glass of the camera's lens, and then we pay cold cash to see it projected upon the screen. And it's that screen, that silver screen, which puts you in the dark. Which separates you from that which brought you into these reclining seats. In the dark, you cannot rewind. In the dark, you cannot see just how the magic's made. You feel the magic, the director's hand, but you do not see.

After I was mugged by those three kids on South Grand, I became afraid. I became afraid I'd never be able to feel safe or look again in the eye another black kid wearing Nikes. *White Fuck,* they called me, taking out my teeth with a chain. But then I went to the dentist, who fixed me—it was only teeth, and my pride, and a car with a hundred thousand miles—and I began to talk to my neighbors, and to their neighbors, and then I met Phoebe who reminded me that anything can happen anytime to anyone, and so knowing that, I became braver. What I'm saying is that at any moment in this life you can meet somebody who will change your life.

As Judy Garland says, bless her ardent heart, There is no place like home.

This is how I proposed to my wife:

I took off for the day, a Tuesday, and showed up at her gallery for lunch, and then I drove us to the Gateway Arch. We went underground to the museum, and because it was a Tuesday, and dead winter, we had no crowds to contend with, and so we took the cantilevered elevator to the top of the arch. Once there, you could feel the wind buffeting the entire structure. You could feel the floors bending beneath our weight as we walked across the platform. Then we stood before the small windows, and I said, That's St. Louis. I wanted, you see, to sell her on the city. I pointed out Union Station, which had become a shopping mall at risk, and I pointed out the

Botanical Gardens, and I said, pointing, There is Washington University.

I said, Here, look.

I offered her a pair of binoculars, which she took. She held them to her eyes and nudged her hip into my side. I said, Look there, and she said, Where? and I said, pointing, There, to a place where I had tacked a small sign to a tree.

Phoebe, it said. *Will you marry me?* _____.

It was the best thing I had ever written—a scene right out of three of my own screenplays; once, I'm told, I almost came close. Still, even with those binoculars Phoebe couldn't read a word of it.

She said, adjusting the focus, What?

And so I translated it for her, and she said, turning, Yes. I think so. But I need to make a trip first.

I held my breath. I stood bravely and told myself I did not look disappointed.

I said, Okay, I can wait.

And she said, I'll leave tomorrow.

Jesus, I said. I'll drive you? To the airport?

No, she said, taking my arm. I just need to do this.

Okay.

We took the ride back down, and located my blue car, and then I dropped her off at her office in the Central West End. I watched the wind catch at her long coat as she walked up the sidewalk alongside Left Bank Books. She pulled open the door to her gallery, turning to smile at me; she brushed the hair from her eyes and stepped inside, and then, the next morning, she called a cab, which arrived in front of her Soulard apartment which I have since loaned out to a refugee family from Srebrenica. At Lambert International, our airport, she walked beneath a small plane which once belonged to Charles Lindbergh, who was first to fly solo all the way to Paris. Phoebe walked beneath Lindbergh's small plane on her way to her gate. The wheels of her carry-on kept catching at the plastic molding on the floors. On her own plane, an antiquated 727, Phoebe leaned back into her seat and took a breath. She thought, Everyplace you go is merely one place along the way to where you're going.

The plane sailed down the runway. The wind, lifting the plane by its very wings, raised it into the air. You can see it, can't you? The plane? It's become the iconic image for our times. At any given moment, there are a quarter million people in the air flying from one destination to another. I thought when Phoebe was sitting back in the plane flying into the sky that she was going off to visit Claire, or the Rock Star, or maybe the Big Wheel at Internet International. I thought maybe there was somebody else I did not know of—which there would be, dozens of others she may have at one time known and loved, being human.

The body does not lie. The first—and the last—thing the body does is take a breath. When I die, I want to be put inside a furnace: I want to go up in flames. The mind may live within our bodies, but our lives are housed within our minds, and this, right now, at this given moment, this is what I'm thinking, stepping inside a cab with my wife beneath the Parisian sky.

It's a warm night. The sky has cleared. When I shut the door, the driver says in his best American, Where to?

I put my arm around my wife and let her provide directions. On the radio, thumping into the sweet insulation of the quiet car, a girl is saying to the music, *I find you very attractive.* The music has a brassy horn thing going on in the distance. Phoebe settles back into the seat, crossing her long legs, and takes my arm. We are feeling bright and sassy, my wife in her new red dress, having dined in a restaurant only the French could possibly devise, and Phoebe says, closing her eyes, and placing my hand beneath the fabric of her dress, Notre Dame.

After disembarking from that flight to Providence, Phoebe went directly to her father and explained that she was prepared to marry a man who sold houses in the dying city of St. Louis. Her father was in the garden, raking leaves, when she arrived; he was wearing brown khakis and a blue sweater full of moth holes. Then he dropped his rake, and took her into his arms, and they stepped into their fine, wooden house through the kitchen, and opened a bottle of wine, and called to her mother who was upstairs making a quilt. Nine months later, the quilt would end up neatly finished across the foot of our bed, and that day, when Phoebe's mother came down the narrow back stairs, her quilting glasses set on her nose, Phoebe told her the news and they sat at the small kitchen table and drank the wine. Then Phoebe called me that night, and asked me to fly out, and on the phone her father asked me questions about where I thought mortgage rates were heading.

When I hung up, the phone rang. Benjamin, telling me he was giving up on the city and reenlisting in the Special Forces.

The army was going to give him several grand as a signing bonus and he was going first to take one of those singles cruises in the Bahamas to spend it. No married women on those boats, he said. No college girls. These women have jobs! He asked me if I was getting any, or not, and if I'd list his condo, and later that night I took my father out to dinner. At Dressel's Pub we ran into Clarence Harmon, who would eventually become mayor of St. Louis, and John Goodman, the actor.

Everywhere you go, my father said, sadly. Everywhere you go people are famous. Bigger than life.

And then I told my father about my plans to marry Phoebe. He liked that news. He walked over to another table, where his friend Leon Strauss was sitting—the developer who saved first the DeBaliviere neighborhood, and then the Fabulous Fox Theatre—and spread the word. Soon everybody was buying me drinks just for getting married, even John Goodman, who bought the house a round, and who as you may or may not know is bigger than life. When things died down, my father returned to our table, and he started talking about things like legacies and grandchildren. After dessert, we discussed then President Bush's decision to go into Somalia, and I remember thinking of Benjamin, M-16 in hand, giving out candy bars to promote democracy, and an equitable distribution of humanitarian aid, and then I told my father about my idea for providing housing to refugees. America was a land of second chances, I explained. It would be good for everybody.

These are empty houses I'm talking about, I said, getting excited. They're going to waste.

St. Louis is good for you, my father said, and we rose and

buttoned up our coats and stepped out onto the street. There were panhandlers sitting in the cold, and my father and I gave them our change, and then I walked my father to his car. I walked my increasingly frail father back to his car because even then I feared for his life.

People used to call my father The Colossus; then he died; and eventually, not that far into the future, there will be nobody left alive to remember the things he said and did. But when I was a boy, he explained to me the history of the world. There are seven wonders to the world, he explained, and there are seven seas to be crossed if you are willing to risk that adventure. You measure the days of your weeks by the seven nights during which you sleep, assuming all is right with the world, beneath the roofs with those you love most. Then my father taught me the constellations in the sky—God's house, the very first, our very own. The place my mother must have filled inside his heart, I don't know how my father survived that loss. The grief our lives were made to bear, it astounds me still.

Be small, my father taught me. Like the seed in a field. Like a star in the sky.

On the lip of this new millennium, nobody knows just yet where we are going to, but I do know that we are going somewhere. As Obi Wan Kenobi advises Luke Skywalker, it's important to use the Force. In our cab, in Paris, the driver grips the wheel with two hands and honks at anybody who comes his way. Eventually, he skids the car into a curb, and across the River Seine, in front of Notre Dame, Phoebe and I exit the cab into the night sky.

Here, I say, taking Phoebe's hand. This way.

We make our way into the park. Inside my pocket is a perfumed piece of paper, which I dip into a birdbath in order to permit the ink to bleed. Sometimes I think there is enough violence in this world to break God's heart, if only He had one, but I've learned to protect myself by loving those I can. The paper dissolves into the color blue, the very color of the sky, and as we make our way beneath the trees into the bower, where we are to be protected by a rooftop of branches and leaves, I breathe in the scent of my wife's perfume. She has placed the perfume behind her ears and along the sides of her throat and between her breasts. The scent blooms off her body like a flower.

I say, I've never done this in public before.

It's only public if people see you, says my wife.

Like a beam of light, I think. Like a candle lit on a dark night, or a lover's kiss. I take off my jacket and spread it across the bench. Phoebe places my hands on her rib cage, then raises them so that I might attend to the buttons on her dress. This way, she says. She undoes my belt and leans me back into the bench and lifts the soft fabric of her dress.

If you disenfranchise the heartland, said Amanda Cunningham Amachi, on CNN, then you disenfranchise the entire population.

I don't know what *disenfranchise* means, but I do know that the heartland is a place within the body and has a constitution all its own. Mostly I think it's the place where my wife's heart beats. It's the place where we raised our daughter into being, and it's the same place where my wife's been leading me ever since we met, all the way to here, right now, to this spot just beneath the sky.

Where to next? Phoebe says, into my ear, her hands on my chest.

In my beginning, wrote somebody else, is my end.

I don't know, I say. A church?

A cathedral, she says. Paradise.

Amen, said Sir Thomas Malory, while writing what would eventually become the story of his life. At the time he had been in prison, and it was dark. Did I tell you that my name is Thomas? Did I tell you that this is the story of my life? A slate, no longer blank, and soon to be erased against Time's very stone. _____. That night I could feel my heart beating against my wife's hands. You get your teeth knocked out, it's easy to think it's never happened to anybody else, but it does, and it will continue to, and the only thing you can do to stop it from happening is to look the other way until you die. All of this is true. Sometimes, sometimes while making love to my wife, I think, This is why God made the world. I think God made the species because he likes to watch us fuck. Do you see what I mean? You see two people who love each other, doesn't it make you feel alive? Doesn't it make your heart brim? I'm not talking about an art film or the soft porn on the late-night cable. I'm not talking about peeping over your neighbor's fence. I'm talking about seeing a man or a woman nudge up against another's body. *O, baby,* Amanda Cunningham used to say, fucking madly in the dark. I'm talking about two people taking each other by the hand. And this is how my wife and I made a girl—and now a boy on the way—who looks like us.

As my father would explain, sadly, this is how it's done everywhere. That night, my wife's hands were all over me; and mine, her—skimming beneath the fabric of her dress, over the surface of her ribs. Stay, they say. *Stay the course.* I could taste the wine on my wife's hot breath. Sometimes I think God must be lonely, not being able to do something so simple and sweet as that. You can be tender, you can be loving, you can be lonely and stupid-drunk or hot as all getout. You can be crazy with grief, delirious with lust. You can be so dizzy you're carried away—by men with handcuffs, or birds of prey. You can be all these things, I think, because that's what you are made of, and God knows that, but He's not allowed to play, because He's God. Zeus, that was a different story, all those heifers and swans. And then I'll think, taking a breath, maybe looking at my wife's pale neck, or the mole on the tip of her mouth, Stop thinking. I'll think that no man alive knows this kind of fierce love until he finds it. And then I'll think that same man ought to stop thinking and simply feel it—the history of the ages, the origins of the cosmos, the mysteries of his universe—and let himself go.

To oblivion, like the seeds in the grass.

ACKNOWLEDGMENTS

These stories first appeared in the following—
"The Gateway" and "Life in the Body" in *Conjunctions*;
"Bastogne" in *DoubleTake*; "Given" in the *Gettysburg Review*;
"Network" in the *Southwest Review*; "Open My Heart" and
"Skin Deep" in the *Yale Review*, the latter reprinted in *Prize
Stories: The O. Henry Awards*.

Thanks be to—
CW @ ASU, One & All; R. C.; Charlie; David Clewell; Chris
C.; Mom & Dad; C. G.; Diane Gilbert; God; Jean & Jerry; Sara
Louise; Matt McNally *et famille*; Michaela; Dear Pam; Kathryn
Lang & The Readers; Patsy (in Spirit); The Brothers & The
Sisters; Sister Susan; Natalie V., who opened the gate —

T, C, & O, who thrice make my heart complete—
T. M. McN.

T. M. McNALLY is the author of five other works of fiction: the novels *Until Your Heart Stops, Almost Home, The Goat Bridge*, and two prize-winning collections, *Low Flying Aircraft* and *Quick*. The recipient of fellowships from the Howard Foundation at Brown University and the National Endowment for the Arts, he teaches at Arizona State University.